I0676262

The City of Lost Secrets

Mara Beltane Mystery Series, Volume 1

Katie McVay

Published by Katie McVay, 2024.

This is a work of fiction. Similarities to real people, places, or events are entirely coincidental.

THE CITY OF LOST SECRETS

First edition. September 14, 2024.

Written by Katie McVay.

PROLOGUE

Jerusalem, Israel
June 2009

The cave was dark and cramped, with less headroom than I had anticipated. I would have to crouch to move around, or crawl on hands and knees.

Once inside the square inner chamber I moved to the east wall and sat on the dusty floor, allowing the dark to envelop me.

He came in after me, flashlight in hand, ready to show me what I had traveled thousands of miles to see.

The flashlight's beam illuminated the loculi that extended out from the main chamber like spokes on a wheel. There were six of these deep niches, two on the east wall behind me, and two each on the north and west walls. The precious contents of the niches had since been removed. Now, every loculi was empty.

Dr. Uri Nevon removed his hat and slid closer to me. "Was this worth the wait?" he asked.

"Absolutely," I said, peering through the dark of the chamber. "So, where was it? Which loculi?"

He shone the flashlight over my left shoulder. "Right behind you."

I hastened to turn around to face the east wall of the chamber, thousand-year-old rock and rubble crunching beneath my feet. Now looking in the right direction, I followed the flashlight beam and peered into the deep niche Uri had been referring to, which at one time had held two small limestone boxes, or ossuaries.

I closed my eyes and pictured one of the ossuaries in particular. In my mind's eye I saw the stray marks that were carved onto the two-foot by one-foot rectangular stone box in various places. There were enough markings to make the ossuary seem significant, but they were oddly and haphazardly placed as if to suggest that someone hurriedly etched them there. To the untrained eye, these marks would look more like primitive

1

graffiti than an ancient inscription. I thought the markings represented letters of some archaic language, perhaps Hebrew.

English is everywhere in Jerusalem but, in the time I spent in Jerusalem, I would grow used to hearing and seeing Hebrew, as well. I heard vendors and passersby yelling it to each other across crowded, chaotic roads; saw signs and street markers and billboards scrawled in its curly-cued alphabet; and, most memorably, listened intently—in a moment of impassioned excitement—as Uri whispered it in my ear.

Ossuaries were nicknamed "bone boxes" because they contained the remains of the dead. This cave, therefore, was a tomb.

I was concerned with one bone box in particular.

"Jesus son of Joseph," I said, reciting the English translation of the inscription on the ossuary that had been my obsession of late, my whole purpose for being here, in Jerusalem, in this tomb.

I looked at Uri, my new Israeli companion. His handsome face was freckled with dirt and his brown eyes were bright with excitement.

"Jesus son of Joseph, Yeshua bar Yosef," he repeated in English and then in Hebrew, the language inscribed on the bone box in question.

We were both silent for a moment, allowing the significance of our surroundings to make its impression on us.

Uri spoke first.

"Welcome to the tomb, the possible final resting place, of Jesus."

CHAPTER ONE

P hiladelphia, Pennsylvania
    May 2009

It was a decent crowd for a rainy Monday night.

Philadelphia, my hometown, was the last stop of my fifth book tour, and I had been hoping for an good turnout.

I was sitting just inside the front doors of a chain bookstore in Center City, behind a table stacked with copies of my newest book, *Heaven Can Wait*, a chick-lit novel about a depressed yet successful bookstore owner named Casey who is visited by an angel. The angel is there to solicit Casey's business savvy. However, Casey thinks the angel is there to take her mother, who is battling breast cancer. Turns out, God's love of all things Gucci has dried up the celestial coffers, and Casey's help is needed to get heaven back in the black.

Ultimately, it's a novel about family and forgiveness and financial responsibility.

Whatever.

It doesn't really matter. All you really need to know is that over the years I've carved out a name for myself as a chick-lit novelist who writes about young, professional, attractive women who experience minor hiccups attempting to find success in life and love.

My novels haven't changed the world, or won any awards, or landed on any best-seller lists, for that matter. I'm not that type of writer. Damn, I wish I was, and I've certainly aspired to be, but I don't know if I have it in me. My talent lies in giving my audience an easy read, a temporary escape, and characters they can identify with.

But I can't complain. My wonderfully talented and shrewd agent, Jenny, took a chance on me, an unpublished author with a passion for writing but with very few writing credits to her name. She liked my writing style and, after years of collaboration, she was helping me publish book number five.

4

And now there I was promoting it. I liked this part of the gig: traveling, meeting new people, connecting with fans.

A red-headed woman who looked to be in her mid-twenties approached the table, and handed me a copy of my book.

"Miss Beltane," she said, "Casey is such a great character."

"Please, call me Mara," I said. "And thank you, I'm glad you think so."

"I was really able to identify with her."

I signed the book and gave it back to her. "That's a relief. I'm always wondering if my characters are relatable enough."

The young woman clutched the book to her and suddenly looked wistful, her eyes glassy with tears.

"Yes, I lost my mom to breast cancer last year," she said. "I'm glad Casey was spared the type of pain I went through. I'm glad you allowed her mom to live."

I was surprised by the confession of this woman and equally filled with admiration for her strength to tell it. She was a literal stranger, and yet I felt the sudden urge to reach across the table and hug her.

"I'm so sorry for your loss," I said.

She smiled wanly. "Thank you."

"Were you close to your mother?"

"Yes and no. We had our moments. But I loved her very much and will miss her the rest of my life."

At that moment I thought about my own mother. We'd had our moments, too. Been through a lot together. What mother and daughter haven't? Images of my trials with my own mother flooded by brain.

When I was a junior in high school my mom snuck into my bedroom and read my diary. On high school graduation day I yelled at my mom and called her weak for seeing a shrink. There was the time she confessed she thought I was making a mistake by marrying Thomas. There was the time she thought I was making a mistake by not having children with Thomas. There was my knowledge of my father's infidelity. There was my father's funeral.

Things worked out more or less okay with my mother, but to this day our relationship is marked by guardedness on both our parts. We bite our tongues instead of speaking to tame our shared conceitedly dogmatic tendencies, and generally agree with each other on everything.

The young woman thanked me for my time and as she walked away I told her that I appreciated her sharing her story. And then I made a note to myself to call two people ASAP: My mother, to tell her I loved her; and Jenny, to suggest that we donate a percentage of the book sales to a breast cancer charity.

Deciding to donate to charity was just the first idea that came to me in a flash in the space of a few days. The next one—a rash, dangerous plan—came the very next day.

At the time, while signing books for fans, I had no idea that in less than seventy-two hours the charity and my conversation with that fan would be relocated to the back of my mind. That's because I'd be far from the city I called home, half-way around the world, in fact, chasing a story and a dream. And in the days and weeks following my return, I'd wonder what would have happened had I stayed in Philadelphia. How different my life might have been if I decided not to get on that plane. If I'd played by the rules.

CHAPTER TWO

"I heard it went well," Jenny asked me on the phone a few days after the Philadelphia book signing.

I was sitting in my living room, curled up on my loveseat, with a program on TV about the extinction of the dinosaurs on mute.

"It went okay," I said, watching as a pair of velociraptors darted across the screen in search of food. "I wish it hadn't been raining. Maybe nice weather would've brought more people out."

"Well, almost fifty people showed up, in spite of the rain. And almost all of them bought at least one of your books."

"Oh, that's more than I thought," I said.

"Overall, the tour did well," Jenny continued. "I've been in contact with each of the bookstore managers and they reported brisk sales and above-average attendance."

"That's great. I'm glad."

"Plus," Jenny continued, "We have the breast cancer charity involvement to look forward to. I e-mailed their information to you."

"Thanks, Jenny. I'll take a look. So since the tour did so well, maybe we should add a few more dates?"

"We could. I'll look into it, if you want."

There is nothing nine-to-five about being a full-time writer. It is an on-going, never-ending attempt to promote yourself and your work. Festivals. Speaking engagements. Book signings. Meetings and phone calls and luncheons with agents and publishers. Late nights. Early mornings. Lots of weekends.

In spite of it all, I love what I do. I wouldn't trade it for anything. And it was my refusal to trade my writing life for one thing in particular that ultimately destroyed my marriage.

"Oh, I almost forgot," Jenny said. "There's a women's writers convention in San Francisco next month. I thought you might be interested. Good networking opportunities. Plus, you know, California."

"That could be fun," I said. "Please send me the info."

Jenny and I said our goodbyes and, bored with the dinosaurs, I started channel surfing.

Should I watch a kitchen remodeling program on HGTV? No, too much of a reminder of the to-do list I had for my townhouse. How about a Phillies game? The home team was just coming off an exciting World Series championship the year before, but I still found baseball to be fairly boring. CNN? Definitely not. I was in no mood for bad news. I finally decided on a program about the exploration of a biblical-era tomb in Jerusalem.

I had missed the first ten minutes, but as it came back from commercial, the narrator recapped what had been covered so far. There's a tomb in Jerusalem that the host of this show believes may be the final resting place of Jesus of Nazareth. The show questions the long-held acceptance of the Church of the Holy Sepulchre being the true site of Jesus' burial because of what was found inside this tomb.

A recreation scene showed how, back in 1980, the tomb was uncovered during a construction project in the Talpiot suburb of Jerusalem. Construction was halted and archaeologists were called in to excavate the area. Artifacts found, including ten ossuaries—or bone boxes—were catalogued and put into storage for safe keeping.

Now the program was displaying some of the ossuaries, including one that the host claimed was inscribed with the words, "Jesus, son of Joseph" in Hebrew. Another ossuary had the name Mary inscribed on it, and the host discussed the possibility of the ossuary belonging to Mary Magdalene.

Was this show suggesting that Mary Magdalene was purposefully interred next to Jesus Christ? For what reason? What could that mean? Suddenly, an idea hit me. An absolutely bat-shit crazy idea...

Images on the television screen flashed in front of me: Jesus secretly kissing Mary Magdalene. Mary Magdalene cradling a baby, presumably her and Jesus' son. Jesus teaching the boy how to work with his hands as Mary Magdalene lovingly looked on in approval from inside their modest Jerusalem home. Then the show faded to a commercial break.

An idea had taken hold in my head and thoughts started swirling around in my brain. I'd been feeling restless lately. I loved novel-writing, but I felt like I needed to do more with it. Like I needed to write something more thought-provoking, more provocative, more challenging.

The last thing Jenny and I had talked about were new book ideas. So that's what I was going to do—throw myself into a new project and get writing again.

And it was going to start right now. By the time I crawled into bed that night, I had formulated my next project and had started researching it.

I knew what I had to do next, and it didn't involve a writer's conference in San Francisco.

I was going to Jerusalem.

CHAPTER THREE

"You're going *where*?" my best friend and old college roommate, Lisa, asked me several days later. We were having lunch at Philadelphia's Reading Terminal Market, an 1893 train station turned farmers market with aisle upon aisle of produce stands and stalls of exotic food and niches filled with everything from used books to bags of sweets. We were sitting at a high counter on swivel chairs, each attempting to finish half of a large cheese steak we were splitting.

"Jerusalem," I repeated, although, in spite of the noise, I knew Lisa had heard me the first time. She was just shocked by the news, as evidenced in the way she played with a strand of her long, straight blonde hair. She said nothing, so I explained to her the TV show that inspired the trip, and the plan for my next novel.

"Huh, that's interesting," Lisa said. "Do you have any connections in Jerusalem?"

"Well, no. But maybe I'll find some experts online and then meet up with them once I get there."

"What kind of experts?"

"Professors, archaeologists, scientists, biblical scholars..."

Lisa took a sip of soda. "And you're going to tell them...what?"

I knew what she was driving at. I was a chick-lit novelist, not an investigative journalist or reporter. I didn't know if I'd be taken seriously, and I wasn't sure if anyone would be willing to talk about this sensitive, controversial subject.

"I don't know yet," I said. "Probably that I'm a journalist working on a book." Both of which were facts. I *was* working on a book, and I had worked a brief stint as a journalist for my local newspaper...albeit many years ago as a young woman right out of college.

"This is a big leap for you, book-wise," Lisa said. "Not to mention that you haven't traveled anywhere since, well, you know..."

"Since Thomas," I said, and she nodded. She was right. I hadn't taken any sort of personal vacation since the divorce. Not even so much as a day trip or weekend jaunt that wasn't related to my professional career.

We were world travelers, Thomas and I. Every year we took one or two international trips. All told we had been to nearly twenty countries together, from Belgium and Greece to Romania and Bulgaria, to China and Japan, to Morocco and Egypt. We were expert travelers and wonderful travel companions. When we weren't traveling, we were talking about travel, or contemplating our next trip, or researching travel destinations.

In the more than a year since the divorce, I'd hardly left Pennsylvania, let alone the country. I was a little rusty, and now I was alone, but I figured with my years of travel experience, I would be just fine on my own in Jerusalem.

"Are you sure you want to do this?" Lisa said. "It sounds dangerous."

"I'll be fine," I said.

Lisa and I had met as freshman in college. We were each other's first and only roommates over the course of four years. Our differences—in everything from choice of clothing to taste in men—had surprisingly drawn us closer together and made us better friends. Probably because we had nothing to fight over. We were the solid Odd Couple, more dissimilar than similar, yet somehow it worked.

Over the course of a twelve-year friendship we'd been each other's rock through everything—breakups, unemployment, illness, divorce, death. We challenged each other's decisions without judgment and knew never to take any response personally.

And the look on Lisa's face in that moment meant a challenge to my decision was coming.

Just then our waitress appeared, cleared our paper plates and trash from the counter, and asked if we wanted anything else. We both shook our heads and she pulled a receipt from her apron, scanned it, then flipped it upside down on the counter.

"Famous last words," Lisa said in response to my comment about being fine in Jerusalem.

"What are you afraid of?" I asked her.

"I mean, I'm just worried about you in general."

"Well, thanks. I appreciate it."

"You've been really busy with your books and the divorce is still kind of fresh..."

"I'm not burying myself in work in order to forget any lingering emotions about Thomas or our marriage."

Lisa handed her credit card and the receipt to the waitress. "Didn't say you were. I'm just making sure you're okay."

"I'm okay. I still see my therapist from time to time and she's helped a lot."

"That's great."

"And this trip, well...I have to go."

"Why?"

"I need to grow as a writer and in order to do that, I need to challenge myself."

"By going to Jerusalem..."

The waitress handed Lisa her credit card back and receipts to sign.

"Aren't there days when you're tired of being a third-grade teacher?" I asked as she figured out the tip and signed both receipts, shoving one into her purse.

"Only every day," Lisa said, laughing.

"Don't you sometimes feel like you need a change, or need to do something different?"

"I always wondered what it would be like to teach abroad."

"You have? I never knew that."

"I've contemplated taking a sabbatical and teaching English or Math to less fortunate international children. Or English as a second language."

"You'd be great at that. You should consider it."

"But I'd have to get it okayed by the school district and uproot my family and leave my friends...." She trailed off. "No offense, it's much easier for you to jet off somewhere in search of new adventures and opportunities."

"I guess it is," I said.

"I know taking the plunge would be great for me on so many levels but...well, it's just not in the cards for me at the moment."

"I understand," I said.

"And I do understand why you need to do what you need to do. You were born to write. You have to go."

"And you have to stay put for now. Otherwise, all your third graders would be stuck with an inferior replacement while you were gone. Now they'll continue to get a quality education."

Lisa smiled and patted my hand and asked, "How long will you be gone?"

We gathered our belongings and made our way through Reading Terminal Market.

"Not sure," I said, as we exited the market and onto the street. "But don't worry. I'll probably be back home in no time."

CHAPTER FOUR

*I*n *1980, a construction crew digging in the East Talpiot district of Jerusalem unearthed a tomb. Construction work on the planned apartment complex was immediately halted and an excavation crew with the Israel Antiquities Authority (IAA)—the government body responsible for the safeguarding of all of Israel's antiquities—was called in to excavate the tomb and recover any treasures that may be buried inside. Ten ossuaries, or stone bone boxes, were found, six of which had names inscribed on them in either Hebrew of Greek.*

The inscriptions read:

Yeshua bar Yosef

Marya

Matia

Yose

Yehuda bar Yeshua

Mariamene e Mara

The bones inside the ossuaries, as well as human remains found inside the cave, were reburied according to Jewish tradition. The ten ossuaries were removed from the tomb and catalogued. The six that bore inscriptions were put into storage in the Beth Shemesh district in north Jerusalem, in a warehouse operated by the IAA.

The four undecorated ossuaries were put in the courtyard of the Rockefeller Museum, where dozens of other similarly undecorated ossuaries were kept on display for the general public.

The tomb aroused no suspicion at the time. Many tombs just like it had been discovered in Israel, and it was deemed to be a typical burial cave of a wealthy, first-century Jewish family. Then, in 2007, a controversial documentary was released, claiming that the Talpiot tomb was the final resting place of Jesus of Nazareth.

I tucked the computer printout back into my carry-on in time for the plane's descent into the Ben Gurion Airport in Tel Aviv. After the long flight I was jetlagged, but had to prepare for an hour-long ride in a *sherut*, or shared taxi, to my hotel in Jerusalem.

The hotel was in the modern part of the city, called New City, a shrimp-shaped area that wrapped around the north and west sides of the Old City, which was the heart of Jerusalem.

After checking into my hotel, I decided to take a walk to start familiarizing myself with Jerusalem.

There'd be time later for exploring the sites. Now was the time to just walk, to absorb the atmosphere around me. If I was to spend productive time in this city researching and writing my next book, I needed to get my bearings. Walking was the only way I knew how to get the lay of the land.

I felt safe walking through the New City. How could I not? There were armed soldiers everywhere, no doubt members of the Israeli Defense Force. They hung around in groups of two or three, all of them in their olive-green jumpsuits and matching berets, with rifles slung over their shoulders. They patrolled the public areas, especially the border gates and passageways leading into and out of the Old City. They wandered the streets talking amongst themselves, and hung around outside the bus stations, waiting for transport to and from their bases.

On this day, in addition to military personnel and Israeli policemen, traffic choked the streets. People of multi-cultural descent scurried along the sidewalks on their way to work and school. Life, in other words, carried on. It was business as usual.

The New City of Jerusalem was appropriately named. It was an area that started being built up during a building boom in the mid-19th century, once the walled areas of the ancient Old City had become overcrowded. The building boom saw the construction of Jewish community projects and a Russian compound for religious pilgrims, as well as the powerhouses of Europe trying to exert their political power and influence through architecture. Hence, English cathedrals and German hospices and Italian office buildings all vied for attention. Most recently, modern art exhibits had been added to the mix, as well as night clubs and high-end glass-and-steel shopping centers.

Before I knew it, I had crossed the boundary of the New City into the ancient roads of the Old City. Two green-outfitted border guards watched as I passed, but otherwise left me alone.

There is a noticeable difference between these two areas. Modern Jerusalem is all business and pleasure. The Old City, however, divided into quarters and walled off from New City, is a mix of commerce and spirituality, with short, cobbled streets that always lead to a place of worship or a shop for tourists or a hospice for pilgrims.

The Old City represents the true history of Jerusalem, 3,000 years of war, occupation, conquest and settlement by the Canaanites, Assyrians, Babylonians, Byzantines, Romans, the Muslims in the East and the Crusaders in Europe and one Alexander the Great. Each had a vested interest in Palestine, a reason for their willingness to fight and die for the land they thought was theirs, rightfully or not. And each culture left its mark in the form of a church, a mosque, a temple, a gate, a public square.

It was this reason, this complicated history, and the fact that the pedestrian Old City is mostly car-free, that made me want to visit this area first.

The Christian Quarter, the area of the Old City where I found myself, was home to one of the most sacred of all Christian sites. Before I knew it I was at the courtyard entrance, staring up at a mosaic of roofs and domes. The Church of the Holy Sepulchre.

A building has existed on this plot of land since the fourth century A.D. Most recently rebuilt in the 20th century, remnants of its past can be seen in the 11th century courtyard, the 12th century addition, and the 18th century bell tower.

It's what's inside that matters most to Christians, though, as this is the supposed site of Christ's crucifixion, burial and resurrection.

As I stood outside the main arched entranceway someone caught my eye: an older gentleman wearing a black robe with a long white beard standing off to the side. I presumed he was of some importance, perhaps a member of one of the Christian denominations that shares custody of this church and other holy places in Jerusalem.

The robed man had a friendly face and smiled at everyone as if to say, "Welcome to my home," but he did not speak. He kept his hands folded in front of him, hidden inside the long, wide sleeves of his robe.

I wondered if he knew the secrets of the building he stood outside, if his membership in organized religion included taking a vow of silence when it came to the truth concerning the death of Jesus. Did he know for sure if Jesus ascended into heaven body and soul and was then resurrected? Or was Jesus simply a flesh and blood human, a simple Jewish man, dedicated to spreading his message of peace and love for all mankind who found himself at the wrong place at the wrong time?

Perhaps the elderly man with the long white beard who stood outside the Church of the Holy Sepulchre had all the answers. Perhaps the true story was handed down to him as a young man by his elders, who, in turn, received the story from their elders, and so forth. Maybe there was an oral history of secrecy dating all the way back to Emperor Constantine, who legalized Christianity in the 4th century, making it the official religion of the Roman Empire.

My most pressing thought at the moment, though, was the building itself, the most important in all of Christendom. Was it really the place of Christ's crucifixion and burial and resurrection? I had my doubts.

I am not a religious person by any stretch of the imagination. Given my preoccupation with going to Jerusalem, I probably give the impression that I was devout at one time, and that maybe some traumatic incident caused me to lose faith and give it up. But I didn't leave any religious faith behind. None had ever existed in the first place.

My parents were Catholic. At least, I assumed they were because of the framed wedding ~~pic~~ that hung in our living room. Mom and Dad, and their bridesmaids and groomsmen on either side of them, all stood in front of an altar, a huge wooden crucifix mounted on the wall behind them. Standing on the step behind my parents was a man wearing a long black robe holding a Bible.

For some reason, my parents never sent me to Sunday school or Bible study classes, and I went to church only a handful of times in my life. So how would I possibly know about Jesus and the saints and the prophets? For the longest time, in fact, I thought God and Jesus Christ were the same person. I had heard of the apostles, but I never understood what they did, exactly, or what Joseph had to do with anything. But the point is, I was no worse off for not knowing. God didn't figure into my life, yet I still turned out okay.

When I did start learning about God at the age of seventeen, however, things suddenly weren't okay for me. The rest of that story is another tale for another time. Needless to say I don't profess to have all the answers. I was here in Jerusalem to write a novel about the death of Jesus. My magnum opus. And if that documentary turned out to be true, that the final resting place of Jesus Christ had been found...well, all the better. That revelation would certainly rock Christianity to its core, almost guaranteeing that the novel I was going to write would be a best-seller.

Finally, at long last, I would give my readers—and the whole world—one hell of a page-turner.

CHAPTER FIVE

O ne of the best ways to learn about a city, other than walking it, is to visit its museums. This is why I decided to visit the Rockefeller Archaeological Museum on my second day in the city. I'd read that this museum housed some wonderful Holy Land antiquities, including some of the Dead Sea Scrolls.

The museum was a short walk from my hotel, down Sultan Suleyman Street. I kept the walls of the Old City to my right and, once I'd reached Herod's Gate on my right-hand side and saw a white limestone building wrapped around a central courtyard on my left across the street, I knew from my guidebook's description that I'd arrived at the Rockefeller Museum.

I had arranged for a private tour of the exhibits with one of the curators. Given that he or she was an employee of the Israeli Antiquities Authority, the same organization that excavated the Talpiot tomb, it would be interesting to see where he or she stood on the matter.

I stepped out of the heat and into the air conditioned lobby and approached the main desk. There were two women standing behind it, conversing in Hebrew. They giggled as if exchanging gossip, but stopped and composed themselves when they saw me walking towards them.

The taller, younger and thinner of the two ladies smiled at me and asked in perfect English, "How may I help you?"

"My name is Mara Beltane," I said, surprised and yet not that the woman knew to address me in English. Surely I looked American to them, dressed as I was in casual attire that included a pair of sneakers, the most American of accessories. I leaned against the cool counter, reflecting briefly on the fact that not only do Americans stick out like sore thumbs abroad, no matter how hard we try to blend in, but that America is one of the few countries whose citizens aren't bilingual. "I have a private tour of the museum scheduled for 10 a.m.," I said.

The two women exchanged looks and nodded at each other. Then the older lady, perhaps fifty or so and plump, stepped out from behind the counter and clasped her hands in front of her. She wore a skirt the color of pink coral that skimmed her knees and a matching blazer. Her low, off-white heels matched the hue of the scarf around her neck, which accented her short, blonde hair.

"Welcome to the Rockefeller Archeological Museum," she said in accented English. "My name is Tovah and I'll be giving you the tour today."

· · · ·

THOMAS AND I VISITED some of the best art museums in the world together: The British Museum; the Rijksmuseum; the Met; The Musee d'Orsay; the Guggenheim; Museo del Prado; the Louvre.

We loved art and everything it represented. I was partial to painting, especially the experimental works of the Impressionists and the spirituality of the Pre-Raphaelites. Thomas had a thing for sculpture, most particularly, Rodin. Our very first date, in fact, had been to the Rodin Museum in Philadelphia.

Thomas respected Rodin (and envied him, I think, although he'd never admitted it) for his ability to create a thing of beauty from a slab of rock. Rodin could mold stone to look like human flesh and manipulate it to portray passion, desperation, love.

Thomas wasn't blessed with any sort of artistic creativity. This haunted him and, I think, ultimately was partially responsible for destroying our marriage. I had my novels, but Thomas never had a creation to call his own.

As the years went by and our museum visits continued, I noticed he'd pause just a little longer at the Madonna and Child paintings of the Renaissance, tilt his head and smile at the family portraits of the 18th century Rococo, step closer as if to feel the fabric of Degas' delicate ballet dancers.

These were the moments, as children stared back at him from two-dimensional canvases, that I think he was realizing there was something he could create after all, one thing that he could call his own: a masterpiece he would be proud to call son or daughter. The years passed and, although I continued to create novels, Thomas's dream of fatherhood was slowly slipping away.

It wasn't until he saw Georges Minne's "Woman Weeping for Her Dead Son" that I think he realized his fate. He walked several times around the late 19th century black stone sculpture, which depicts a young boy laying limp and lifeless in his mother's arms as she stretches her neck skyward in agony over her loss. I drifted off to view the other pieces in the room. He didn't notice when I returned to his side a few moments later, not even when I touched his arm. He continued to stare at the woman and her dead boy as I slipped my hand into his, sure that that would awaken him from his melancholy trance. When it did not, I recoiled my hand, feeling that Thomas had somehow become a part of the sculpture during my brief absence. The intense sadness in his eyes, the slight hunch of his shoulders…If not for the warmth of his hand I'd have sworn he'd turned to stone as well.

For a moment I wasn't Thomas's wife, but a stranger walking in on an intimate scene between a man and a woman and their moment of shared grief. My sudden panic—the feeling of being alone, of thinking I'd lost him—made me take a step back. I couldn't bear to be that near to him knowing that he was not mine, as brief as the moment was.

Thomas finally turned to me, when he'd decided he no longer wanted to be a part of the sculpture, when he no longer wanted to think about the lost child. He had a mist in his eye that I hadn't seen before or since, not even as our marriage crumbled and separation became the only way to ease his bitterness and disappointment. At that moment, in a museum in Brussels, Thomas was mourning the child he'd never have.

It was one of the last trips we took together. I had denied Thomas his chance to create something special, something beautiful. He said he felt my writing career was more important to me than he was. He thought I didn't care about his desire to become a dad. There was a resentment I could not bear.

Several months later we were going through the process of being legally separated. We sold the house we had shared together for seven years and each got a place of our own. We e-mailed or texted back and forth for awhile, whenever little things needed to be resolved, like when we found things that belonged to each other: Thomas' old Penn sweatshirt. A sketchbook filled with my writings. CDs. Books. DVDs.

Eventually the communication stopped altogether and then there was silence. That was more than a year ago.

It was hard not thinking about Thomas as Tovah led me from room to room through the museum. Each exhibition hall we toured resembled a cathedral, a cathedral Thomas and I had visited together: long rooms with high ceilings and impossibly large windows to allow for natural light. All the cathedrals and churches we visited came back to me in a rush of memories as we moved from hall to hall: Karlskirche in Vienna, where we saved twelve Euros by not going inside because we decided this Baroque church couldn't possibly be any more beautiful on the inside than it was on the outside. St Paul's Cathedral in London, which we decided was worth the price of admission so we could climb the 259 steps to the Whispering Gallery, and another 371 steps to the summit for the extraordinary view of the city. Notre Dame in Paris, where, in order to recover from the sheer beauty and magnificence of the rose windows, we sat on a nearby park bench and shared a crepe drenched in chocolate.

As Tovah led me from one exhibition hall to another, I imagined he was there with me. Thomas was suddenly by my side, inside the Rockefeller Museum. He smiled and took my hand as the tour guide said that this museum was the first in the Middle East to make a systematic collection of finds from the Holy Land. Tovah then mentioned the Dead Sea Scrolls and I muttered Thomas's name and turned to him to say that we must see them before we leave...and saw only the tour guide, looking at me curiously.

Suddenly I was alone once again. The idea of Thomas had vanished, leaving me alone with my guilt and anguish and pity. Tovah narrowed her brown eyes at me and asked if I was okay, if I wanted to sit down or was in need of a restroom, to which I smiled and asked when I'd get to see the Dead Sea Scrolls.

"The Dead Sea Scrolls are housed at our nearby sister Museum, the Israel Museum, in a building called the Shrine of the Book," Tovah said, a look of concern still on her face. "Your admission ticket is good for that museum as well. There's a free shuttle bus that'll take you there."

Certainly, absolutely, I would take the shuttle over to the other museum. But first I had to remind myself of two things: First, that my time of touring the world with Thomas was over, and that he was, in fact, gone from my life, perhaps forever. And second, that I was in Jerusalem for a reason, and could not allow nostalgia to rob me of this important opportunity. I had two hours alone with a museum curator who had vast knowledge of biblical history and archeology. I'd be remiss not to ask her for information about the Talpiot tomb.

Tovah led me back into the lobby. She thanked me for coming, encouraged me to visit the gift shop, and asked if I had any questions.

"Yes, I do," I said, looking around at the visitors milling around the lobby and scurrying every which way to the various exhibition halls. The museum was more crowded than when I'd entered nearly two hours before. I turned my head slightly in the direction of the entrance doors and saw out of the corner of my eye a tour bus outside unloading its passengers. In a matter of moments the large group would descend on the lobby, making conversation more difficult. I had to act quickly, especially if this group was Tovah's next responsibility.

"I...I saw a documentary recently about a tomb found on the outskirts of Jerusalem. Do you know which tomb I'm talking about?"

"Well, there are tombs all over Jerusalem," Tovah said, folding her hands in front of her again. "In fact, this museum was built on the site of Hellenistic and Byzantine-era graves. Construction was halted for some time in order for them to be excavated."

"The tomb in this documentary was older," I said. "It dated from the time of Jesus. I'm trying to remember the name."

"I'm sure I don't know," Tovah said.

"Talpiot!" I said, as if the name suddenly came to me. "The Talpiot tomb! That's what it's called."

The smile melted from her face. "The Talpiot tomb?"

"Yes, it was uncovered in 1980, I think, and some say it is the lost tomb of Jesus of Nazareth."

"I'm familiar with what is being said about it," she said, shifting on her feet.

"Have you seen the documentary? It claims that Jesus was not resurrected, and that he was married to Mary Magdalene and they had a child, and that the Talpiot tomb and the ossuaries found inside are the proof."

Tovah cleared her throat. "I might have seen it. I can't recall."

"All those ossuaries pulled from the tomb bore inscriptions of names who were members of Jesus' family. That's pretty incredible."

Tovah shook her head. "Four of the ossuaries had no inscription. And to say that the remaining six must have belonged to Jesus' family is a stretch. They were all very common names at the time. For example, one of the ossuaries bore the inscription Mary. Twenty-five percent of women in Jerusalem at the time were named Mary."

The common name theory. From what I'd read, it seemed to be the most popular explanation among scientists and scholars debunking the Talpiot tomb.

"But do you think that's enough evidence to discredit the claim?" I asked, glancing outside again at the bright, sunny day. All of the passengers had disembarked from the bus, and the bus was pulling away. Some of the passengers were fanning themselves against the late morning heat.

"The IAA's stance is that neither the Talpiot tomb nor the ten ossuaries found inside are extraordinary," Tovah said.

"The IAA?" I asked, returning my attention back to her.

"The Israel Antiquities Authority," she said. "It's the government agency responsible for controlling and protecting Israel's treasures. They also run this museum and our sister museum, the Israel Museum. So as a curator of this museum, I am also an employee of the IAA."

"I understand that, and I'm familiar with the IAA," I said. "But I'd really like to know how you personally feel about the Talpiot tomb."

"Why?"

"I'm just...curious."

Tovah eyed me for a brief moment longer before answering. "The Talpiot tomb is a typical first-century Jewish burial cave. Hundreds of tomb caves just like it have been found in Jerusalem and the vicinity."

"So, in your opinion, it's not the tomb of Jesus Christ?" I asked.

"Jesus' family was from Galilee and had no ties to Jerusalem, so there is little likelihood that this is the tomb of Jesus and his relatives."

"But Jesus died here," I said. "The New Testament tells us what happened to his body. He was buried here, and, Christians believe, resurrected here. How can you say there were no ties to Jerusalem?"

"No *family* ties," Tovah said, shifting on her feet again. "Other than Jesus, who?"

"Well, we know from the Gospel of Mark that Jesus' brother James lived and died in Jerusalem, so there's a family tie," I said. "Is it such a stretch to suggest that Jesus' family relocated here from Galilee, and was therefore buried here?"

"No, that is not a stretch," Tovah said. "But to suggest that the Talpiot tomb specifically, with ossuaries etched with the most common names at the time, is the burial cave of Jesus of Nazareth is a stretch."

Our conversation had come full circle.

"The common name theory is well documented and seems to make sense," I said. "But just because I'm originally from Philadelphia doesn't mean I'll be buried in Philadelphia."

"You can't compare the funerary practices of different religions and different time periods to prove your argument. That is, as you might say, comparing apples to oranges? Jews in first-century Jerusalem practiced secondary burial: bones of the deceased were removed from a first grave and then placed in an ossuary and buried in a familial cave near the family's geographic origins."

"You said there was 'little likelihood' that the Talpiot tomb was the tomb of Jesus," I said. "But you didn't say there was *no* likelihood. So you're not completely convinced?"

Tovah smiled. "Miss Beltane, if you are trying to get me to confess to something I do not believe, you are out of luck."

Voices started filling the lobby. The tour group was making its way inside. I turned my head and saw the tour leader waving a red flag attached to a long stick, herding her flock. I didn't have much time left.

"If only the ossuaries were researched further," I said. "Maybe then you'd—"

"We don't find the ossuaries to be worthy of further research," Tovah interjected, raising her voice to compete with the influx of noise.

"If they're not worthy of further research, then why are they locked up in a warehouse in Beth Shemesh?" I asked. "Why aren't they on display for the general public to see?"

"The ossuaries are old and fragile and...in need of protection, shall we say."

"Protection?" I asked, surprised by her choice of words. "From what?"

"Miss Beltane, Israel has seen enough fighting. My country doesn't need another battle on its hands."

"Battle?" I said.

Tovah ignored my question, motioning instead to the tour group that was mingling in the corner by the entrance. "If you'll excuse me, I have another tour."

"Of course," I said.

"It was a pleasure meeting you, Miss Beltane," Tovah said. "Enjoy the rest of your stay, and good luck with whatever business brings you to Jerusalem."

Then Tovah walked away, back towards the counter where we'd first met, and to a group of tourists who would, no doubt, never know about our Talpiot tomb conversation, if they knew about the Talpiot tomb at all.

CHAPTER SIX

The next day I found myself in the Old City, walking through a small and touristy souk. All around me shops and stalls were filled with racks overflowing with scarves, rugs, shoes, and religious trinkets. Tables lined the path on both sides, overflowing with even more souvenirs: books, cheap magnets, stationary, handbags. English, Hebrew and Arabic were shouted all at once, as tourists haggled for that perfect find with local merchants who were searching for the best price for their wares. The aisle was narrow and as I struggled to push my way through the throngs of people, I occasionally had to turn sideways to pass, mumbling an apology the few times I accidentally bumped into someone.

To compound my discomfort was the thick air, filled with the scent of spices and incense so intense that I was sometimes forced to hold my nose against their dizzying intoxication. And the heat! Surely I'd never felt any fever as powerful as this, the result of a blazing Middle Eastern sun in May.

I was careful not to make eye contact with any vendor or pause too long at any one stall, lest I find myself invited in for a closer look. I was not here to shop, after all; I was simply looking for a shortcut through the Old City en route to the Mount of Olives.

The Mount of Olives overlooks Old City to the east, and most visitors climb its summit for the breathtaking view. I, on the other hand, wanted to go there for an entirely different reason. The Mount of Olives, along with Mount Zion to the west, is where Jesus spent his last days, and it was important for me—for the novel I was going to write—to walk in his shoes.

But at the moment I was walking through a souk, and I was distracted—by the heat, by the intense noise, by the stench that was meant to lure visitors...and by the conversation I'd had yesterday with Tovah at the Rockefeller Museum. She had been hesitant to give her personal opinion of the Talpiot tomb at first, answering in the plural. *We* don't think the tomb is worthy of further research. *We*, as in the IAA, her employer, the agency that was responsible for excavating the Talpiot tomb back in 1980. The same agency that is now housing the six inscribed ossuaries that were found in the tomb in a warehouse outside of Jerusalem.

When I pressed her further, however, Tovah made it very clear that she didn't think the Talpiot tomb was the final resting place of Jesus Christ. My research indicated that most people shared her opinion. So, while Tovah told me what I needed to hear, I certainly had not made a friend or earned her trust.

I wanted to believe the Talpiot tomb was real, that the final resting place of Jesus Christ had been found. It would be the perfect scenario for the novel I was attempting to write. But I needed to confirm it.

Was Jesus married to Mary Magdalene? Did they have a child? Were they all buried together, along with other family members, in a family cave on the outskirts of Jerusalem? Could all that possibly be true? The makers of the documentary that inspired my trip to Jerusalem think so, and went so far as to hint at a conspiracy to cover up the truth.

So, as I walked through the crowded pathway of the souk, glancing fleetingly at the faces of the people who knew and loved Jerusalem best, I wondered: would anyone come forward and admit they believed the Talpiot tomb was the real deal? Perhaps Tovah's response was just the first of many disappointments I would face as I attempted to discover the truth.

This was bore out by the fact that my emails to carefully researched Jerusalem-based scholars and professors had gone unanswered. I had come to Jerusalem empty-handed but undeterred, with nothing but an idea and a dream to guide me.

The heat of the day was starting to get to me, as was the atmosphere of the market, so as I emerged from the souk I decided to duck into a small, air-conditioned store for a few minutes of quiet, cool relief. There were no other patrons and the shopkeeper was nowhere to be found, but the bell that chimed as I entered the store would surely cause him or her to emerge eventually. I took the brief moment alone to catch my breath and look around.

The store's carpet was the color of midnight and the walls were white, with blue and teal and green geometric patterns painted like tiles around the perimeter. There were several glass display cases in the middle of the store, as well as shelves mounted on the walls that held everything from copper and brass eating and drinking vessels, to beauty products, to silver jewelry. A service counter stood against the back wall straight ahead of me.

My eye was drawn to a display of olive wood objects on a shelf to the left of the entry door. The light-colored wood items were intricately carved figures of Christ and the Virgin Mary, as well as nativity scenes and crucifixes. I bent over and picked up an olive wood rosary, which I thought would make a nice gift for my mother. It was just about then that I heard rustling behind me.

"Hello, welcome!" a male voice said.

I stood up, startled, and turned to see a tall, scrawny boy, perhaps eighteen or twenty years old. He had dark brown eyes framed by glasses and cropped black hair. He was wearing a green and white striped pull-over collared shirt that hung over a baggy pair of jeans.

"Hello," I said.

"First time to Jerusalem?"

"Yes."

"Are you here for business or pleasure?" His English was perfect.

"A little of both, I guess."

"I figured. Most women don't travel here alone for personal reasons. Especially American women."

"No, I suppose not," I said, surprised at his honesty.

"Men might stare at you, and possibly taunt you," he warned. "Just be careful." Then he shrugged.

I'd read as much in my guidebook, but thankfully I had had no encounters so far.

"Thanks for the tip," I said.

The boy smiled, then motioned to the rosary I still held in my hand. "Good choice. All of our olive wood pieces are from Bethlehem. The best that money can buy."

"You work here?" I asked, and the boy nodded. "It's beautiful. But I'm not looking to buy anything today."

"We carry gifts for the whole family. If you don't see what you're looking for here, I bet I could find it for you elsewhere."

I placed the rosary back on the shelf. "Thank you."

As I started to walk past him to leave the store, he reached his hand out in introduction.

"My name is Lev."

"Oh, uh...Mara," I said, hesitantly taking his hand.

"Well, Miss Mara, is there something that you're looking for?"

There certainly was, but he'd probably never heard of the Talpiot tomb and therefore couldn't help my mission. But I decided to stay, because he was very nice and had kind eyes.

"Well...not really," I said.

"Not really?"

"It's...complicated. What I'm looking for."

"Please, tell me. Perhaps I can help."

Ah, the hell with it.

"I'm looking for....I'm looking for a tomb," I said.

"A....tomb?"

"An ancient tomb. On the outskirts of town. It was discovered almost thirty years ago, but apparently it's covered up now..."

Lev's eyes grew large behind his glasses and he shrank back a few steps. "Are you with the police?"

"The police? Of course not."

"A reporter, then?" He appeared visibly shaken.

"Not exactly. Look, did I upset you?"

He looked at me a moment, silent. Finally, he said, "I know why you're here."

"You do?"

"Of course," he said, and walked behind the service counter. "The Talpiot tomb."

"You've heard of it?"

"Yes. There was a documentary about it. I already knew about the tomb, though. The documentary created a controversy. People went crazy!"

"I've seen the documentary."

"Most people don't believe any of it."

"What do you think?"

Lev eyed me suspiciously. "Who are you?"

"Nobody," I said. "I'm nobody."

"What do you want?"

"Nothing. I'm just curious about the tomb."

"You said you were *looking* for the tomb."

I stood there a moment, wondering how I could escape further suspicion, and not further upset the young local.

When I said nothing, Lev busied himself with some paperwork on the counter. "I'm sorry, Miss Mara. If I don't know who you are, I won't be able to help you."

I couldn't just leave. The suspicion in the young man's eyes and in his voice. The way he backed away from me, asked if I was with the police. He was scared. He knew something.

"Your English is impeccable," I said finally. "Did you learn that in school?"

Lev didn't look at me. He continued scanning pages of text with a pen as he spoke.

"Yes, English is our second language. You'll find almost everyone in Jerusalem speaks it. Children learn it in school from a very early age."

I wondered how old he was. Lev had an appearance that made deciphering his age a challenge. He had the deep voice of a man, the lanky frame of an adolescent, and the smooth face of a young boy.

"Are you still in school?" I asked.

"I'm in my first year at Hebrew University. I'm studying business."

"What are your plans?"

He looked up from his paperwork. "Plans?"

"Yes, what do you plan to do with your business degree?"

"I will take over this store from my father when it is time," Lev said, returning his attention to the paperwork in front of him. "Other than that, I don't know."

"And you'll take over this shop by choice, or obligation?"

"I feel it is my duty to follow in my father's footsteps, plus I like it. So I study business."

If I wanted to find out what Lev knew about the Talpiot tomb, if I was going to ask for his help, I would have to help *him* in return.

I walked over to the shelf where I'd admired the olive wood trinkets, grabbed the nicest rosary, and made my way back towards the counter. I placed the rosary gently on the service counter, on top of Lev's paperwork, directly under his nose.

The young Israeli boy looked up from his paperwork.

"Do you gift wrap?" I asked.

"That depends, Miss Mara."

"On what?"

"Are you going to tell me who you really are?"

CHAPTER SEVEN

I was devasted, yet not surprised, when Thomas told me he wanted a divorce. I had, in fact, seen it coming.

It was a year and a half ago. I was in the midst of writing my third novel. Thomas came home from work one day and announced, while I was cooking dinner, that we needed to talk.

My fork shook as we ate because I knew, after so many years of dancing around the subject, he was finally ready to tell me: He was unhappy, he didn't feel supported, I wasn't giving him the one thing he truly wanted.

He'd hinted at it for several years, little comments here and there. But, perhaps out of kindness or his own guilt or both, a full confession never materialized.

Not that a full confession would've saved the marriage. It just would've sped up the inevitable. Spared us from years of simmering tension. Allowed us to usher in sooner all the feelings of guilt and anger and resentment and shame and failure.

"I think it's best we go our separate ways," he'd said.

"Is there someone else?" I asked, knowing full well there wasn't, but secretly hoping there was. Because to me, infidelity was way easier to deal with then my own inabilities as a wife. Infidelity was on him. But not wanting to give him kids was on me. Thinking that way made me feel like an awful human being, but the hurt of him wanting to leave pushed me there.

"You know that's not what this is about," Thomas had responded.

So while Thomas claimed it was because I didn't want children, I think it was more than that. I think it was because I had already had children, of a sort. Without him.

My novels absorbed so much of my time. When I wasn't teaching or grading papers or spending time with Thomas (which, admittedly, was less and less as time went on) I was writing frantically on my laptop, or editing, or researching, lost in the world I had created, for hours on end. At those times I was unreachable, unreliable, non-communicative.

Thomas was supportive in the beginning; writing was my true passion and he said I must make time for it, to prove myself in the industry, even if it meant that he had to pick up the slack. But as time went on—as I published my first book and then the second and was embarking on the third—he grew more and more weary, upset by my mental absences, frustrated by the long publicity tours, and now no longer willing to pick up the slack.

Meanwhile, he had needs that were going unmet.

Thomas was already upset that I wasn't giving him enough of my time, and now he wanted to add children to the mix? There was no way I could balance it all. I didn't want to balance it all. I'd decided motherhood just wasn't for me.

I told Thomas all this. We fought about it. He said he'd take on more of the responsibilities. Meanwhile, the idea of children was a conversation we should've had long before marriage, like the moment we started dating.

Sure, he would've supported me in the beginning, taken on the additional duties of being a father, while also being a husband to a neurotic writer. But after awhile he would've grown weary, just like he did when I started gaining success as a writer. He'd grow to resent me and my career. I knew him well enough to know that that would happen. I would've given him what he wanted, children, and it still wouldn't be enough.

My books had become my children. Since he had no part in their creation, and since he had no claim to them, he was threatened by their existence. He sensed my need to produce books was greater than my desire to produce children. And he believed, correctly, that I probably couldn't give it all up if he asked me to. So he didn't ask. After five years of marriage, he decided to leave rather than force me to make that decision.

So when Lev, the young Israeli shopkeeper, asked me who I was and what I wanted, what was I to tell him? That I was a successful writer but a failure as a wife and I was in Jerusalem to reinvent my career because it was the only thing in my life I felt I could reinvent?

How was I supposed to explain to Lev that even though we were strangers I needed his help? And that his help might require an element of danger and put his personal safety at risk? It was ridiculous, really. How stupid, how selfish of me to think he would even consider such a thing. But I had to come up with something quick, because the young Israeli boy was standing in front of me, asking what my intentions were.

"Where are you from?" Lev asked.

"Philadelphia," I said. "Have you been to the States?"

"No, but I want to. New York City, Boston, Los Angeles, maybe Philadelphia. What do you do there?"

"I'm a—"

I was about to tell a white lie, alter my profession, become the journalist I'd told myself I could morph into because I was far enough away from home to get away with it. My "credentials" would enhance my trip, I thought, give me access to people and places that would otherwise be denied to me. But looking at the young man in front of me, the one who'd already proven he was leery of journalists, I decided that I could not, in fact, get away with an identity transformation. My conscience, and, suddenly, reason, wouldn't allow it. Because one lie would beget a second, which would produce a third, until finally I'd become someone I didn't recognize anymore. That would be harmless for transient relationships in Jerusalem, (even though I didn't want to lie to anyone) but people I hoped would become friends and trusted partners? Best to leave the fiction in my novels.

"I write novels," I said.

"What type of novels?" he asked, ringing up my purchase.

"Novels for women."

"Like romance novels? The kind with half-naked people on the cover? My sister reads those."

"No, not exactly. Mine are less racy. They're mostly about single young women in their twenties and thirties trying to succeed in life and love."

"Oh, okay."

"But the new book I'm writing is a departure from what I'm used to. It's a mystery novel about the Talpiot tomb. I'm hoping to attract a broader audience."

"Sounds interesting," he said. "Two hundred shekels, please."

I handed Lev the exact amount, which equaled about fifty U.S. dollars. He put the money in the cash register and dashed behind a blue-curtained opening behind the service counter. He re-emerged carrying a small box, wrapping paper, tape and scissors.

"Oh, you don't have to gift-wrap it," I said. "I was joking. Besides, I'd never get a wrapped box past Customs."

Lev nodded in agreement and reached under the counter for a bag. He gently put the rosary in the plastic bag and handed it to me.

"Are you going to say in your novel that the Talpiot tomb is the final resting place of Jesus Christ?" he asked.

"Yes, I think so," I said, folding the plastic bag and placing it inside my shoulder bag.

"And you're here to do research, talk to experts, find out if it's true?"

"I've come here to do research, and I also want to see the ossuaries for myself." I left out the part about wanting to see the actual tomb. Best not get ahead of myself.

Lev eyed me, sizing me up, perhaps, trying to see if I was serious and sincere. Finally he said, "Uri Nevon."

"What?"

"Dr. Uri Nevon," Lev clarified. "You need to talk to him."

I immediately went for my bag and pulled out my notebook. "Who's he?" I asked, rummaging for a pen.

"He teaches religion classes at Hebrew University."

Finding a pen, I wrote the name down in my notebook. "Do you know Dr. Nevon?"

"I took one of his classes recently. History of Early Christianity. You can find him in the Humanities Department."

"Why should I talk to him?" I asked, jotting down more notes as Lev spoke.

Lev leaned across the counter as if to share a secret. "Professor Nevon seems to know more than anybody about the Talpiot tomb. Some would say he's obsessed."

"Why would people say that?"

Lev shrugged. "They don't understand the passion he has for his line of work, and his country's history."

"So you don't think he's obsessed."

"No. He's a passionate man. Passion can sometimes be confused for obsession."

It struck me how mature a statement that was for such a young person.

"Has he...has he seen the tomb?" I asked.

There was a pause, a moment of silence when neither of us spoke. Finally, Lev said, stammering, "I...well, um..."

"I'll take that as a yes?" I asked slowly.

Lev sighed deeply. "Yes..." Then his eyes grew wide. "But you can't let on that you know!"

"Don't worry," I said evenly, even though I felt like my insides were about ready to burst through my skin. "Your secret is safe with me."

"Thank you."

I might have sounded nonplussed, but my mind was off and running. I was already thinking about what I was going to tell this Dr. Nevon when I met him, and enacting a plan as to how I was going to get inside the Talpiot tomb.

"Did Dr. Nevon talk about the tomb in class?" I asked.

"Oh, no," Lev said. "Never."

"Why not?"

"Miss Mara, you must know that the tomb is off limits. It's been sealed up for a long time."

"Yes, I've read that."

"Admitting that you've seen the Talpiot tomb isn't something you advertise. He hadn't been invited. What he did was dangerous! What we...I mean, what he did was illegal."

He didn't think I heard him but I did.

We. What *we* did.

I had one final question for the boy.

"Lev, if the professor never talked about the Talpiot tomb in class, then how do you know he's seen it?"

Lev shrank back. He had said too much and he knew it. But then his body relaxed and he smiled, a devilish look in his eye.

"Miss Mara," he said, grinning, "who do you think got him inside?"

CHAPER EIGHT

Dr. Uri Nevon is a biblical scholar and historian, and a professor of biblical history courses at Hebrew University. He has given lectures at Harvard and Yale in the United States, as well as other colleges and universities around the world. He frequently contributes to biblical journals, and has authored two books, "Women of the Bible" and "The Case of the Missing Gospels." He studied Jewish and biblical history at Bar Ilan University in Tel Aviv, where he earned a bachelor's degree. He also holds a Master's in Education (M.Ed.) and a Doctorate in Archeology and Ancient Near East from Hebrew University.

I looked up from the bio I had printed from the Internet and down at the room laid out in front of me. The lecture hall was almost full. Students scribbled furiously into notebooks and some typed on laptops.

The professor paced in front of the long white board as he spoke, his hands clasped behind his back. It seemed at times as if he was talking to himself instead of a room full of students, until a hand went up or someone asked a question. Then the professor stopped dead in his tracks, searched the room for the inquiring student and went to him or her. He would stand beside or in front of the student, address the question at hand, and when he was sure the question was answered fully and they could move on, he resumed his pacing at the front of the room. It was an odd way to lecture, but an effective one, as not one student seemed to lose interest or nod off the entire hour, and only once did a cell phone go off. I even found myself, ten minutes in, reaching into my bag for my notebook in order to take notes.

Dr. Nevon wore loose-fitting khaki pants and a faded, dark blue blazer overtop of a light-blue button up shirt. He had short-cropped brown curly hair, dark eyes and a prominent nose. A few gray hairs around the temples led me to believe he was a little older than me. Forty, perhaps.

I sat in the top row in the far left hand corner of the room.

A hand shot up in response to a statement Professor Nevon was making about the Twelve Apostles. It belonged to a female student near the front row with short, bobbed hair.

"Professor, what about Mary Magdalene?" she asked. "Was she considered an Apostle of Jesus?"

Dr. Nevon walked over to the student and was about to address the issue when another student spoke up, a boy seated several rows behind her.

"Why don't you ask the professor what you really want to know?" he asked, mockingly, as if he knew the girl, and her gossipy proclivities, well.

The girl whipped around in her seat and shot him a glare. "Which is?"

"Were Jesus and Mary Magdalene lovers?" the young man asked, drawing out the word 'lovers.'

There were giggles and snickers from a few of the students.

"Is that what you wanted to know?" Dr. Nevon asked, directing his attention back to the female student. "If Jesus and Mary Magdalene had a relationship beyond that of just teacher and disciple?"

"Well, I guess..." the female student said, squirming in her seat. "I mean, I've heard what-if scenarios about them being married and having a child."

"The simple answer to that question is, we don't know," the professor said, addressing the entire class. "The gospels don't say much about Mary Magdalene, let alone her relationship with Jesus. The early Christian church branded her as a prostitute. Through the centuries she has constantly been reinvented. She is such a mystery that we may never know her true identity. Or we'll never be *allowed* to know."

The same male student who had antagonized the female student raised his hand. He ignored the implication made by the professor and went straight to the gutter.

"You mean there's a possibility that they were gettin' it on?" he asked.

At this, there were chuckles and snickers and sideways glances among the students.

The professor shook his head, smiling, as if to say, "kids will be kids."

As the noise died down the female student raised her hand once again.

"Certainly the Talpiot tomb has some answers to give," she said. "Right, professor?"

The whole room fell silent. I sat up straighter in my chair, surprised by the mention of the Talpiot tomb.

Lev had said Uri never spoke about having seen the Talpiot tomb. Did this student know that he had gained access? And if so, how did she find out? Or had she simply heard a rumor and was hoping he'd confess?

Dr. Nevon smiled and stared at the floor a moment, probably wondering how to address the sudden change of subject.

"Perhaps it does," he said finally. "And one day we may know the truth. Until then, the mystery lives on..."

A few of the students exchanged curious glances, and the room remained silent, waiting for the professor to offer more. But he didn't. He returned to the front of the class and resumed pacing, launching into a new discussion on another one of Jesus' Twelve Apostles.

Before I knew it an hour had passed and the professor was dismissing the class. I waited until the last student had left the classroom before approaching him.

"Dr. Nevon?" I said, walking down the steps towards the front of the classroom. There was a lectern in front of the white board, and the professor stood at it, loading papers into his briefcase.

"Yes?" he said, not looking up from his briefcase.

"May I have a moment of your time?"

His personal affects finally in order, he raised his head, prepared to deal with whoever was inquiring after him. He set his eyes on me, not unlike the way he looked at his students when they asked a question: deep in the eyes, brows slightly arched in preparation to listen, mouth set squarely.

Up close, I was able to see more of his features: fine lines around the eyes, a thin, yet well-defined nose, a chiseled jaw line. He was, I decided, quite handsome.

The expression on his face changed from inquisitiveness to confusion.

"Are you a student of mine? I don't recall seeing you in class."

"No, I'm not a student here."

He gave me a sly smile. "Does that mean you snuck into my class?"

"Guilty."

"With what intentions?"

"Research. For a book I'm writing."

"What's the topic?"

"Well, the Talpiot tomb...which, coincidentally, one of your students just mentioned."

The professor spoke softly, as if more to himself than to me. "Yes, once in a while someone brings that up in class." He sighed.

"I'd like to talk to you about it. About the Talpiot tomb, I mean."

The professor took his briefcase off the lectern as if preparing to leave. "Is that why you're here, Miss..."

"Mara Beltane," I said, holding my hand out. "I'm sorry. I should have introduced myself."

The professor shook my hand. "Don't apologize. Do you live in Jerusalem?"

"No, I live in the U.S."

"And you say you're writing a book about the Talpiot tomb?"

"I'm writing..." I started, but couldn't finish what was going to be a lie. I was going to tell the professor the same white lie I had prepared for Lev—that I was an American journalist looking to write a non-fiction book about the tomb and the controversy surrounding it. But my better judgement kicked in.

"I'm writing a novel. That's my profession back home. I'm a full-time novelist."

"Oh, I see..."

"I knew I'd be coming to Jerusalem for research, so I did a search on local biblical scholars and your name came up."

"What made you think I'd know anything about the Talpiot tomb?"

"Oh, well..." He had me there. "It became international news when it was discovered, right? So I guess I just assumed most biblical experts would have some insight about it."

The professor thought a moment. "I can try to answer your questions." He opened his briefcase and handed me a business card. "Call or email me and we'll schedule a time to talk."

He shifted on his feet, as if he was about to excuse himself and leave. But I wasn't ready to let him go. Sure, I could schedule an appointment, but Dr. Nevon was here right now. Introductions had been made, and as long as I wouldn't be interfering with this schedule, I wanted to get started as soon as possible.

"Do you have time now?" I asked. "I only have a few questions..."

The professor looked at his watch. "I suppose I have a few minutes before my next class." He motioned for us to sit down in the front row of seats.

I pulled my notebook and pen out of my bag and thought about how I would begin my line of questioning. I was able to let on that I assumed he *knew* about the tomb, but I had to pretend that I didn't know he'd already gained access to it.

"How familiar are you with the Talpiot tomb?" I asked.

"I was a young boy when it was discovered," he said. "It made the news, but ancient tombs and artifacts are discovered here frequently, so it was not that big of a deal."

"At least, not at the time."

The professor laughed. "Right. Not at the time. The Talpiot tomb is from the first century, and is rather common for a middle-class Jewish family living at that time. So at the time of its discovery, it was just another tomb."

"And the ossuaries found inside?"

"Ten in all," Dr. Nevon confirmed. "Six inscribed, four un-inscribed."

"I must ask you about the names etched on the six inscribed ossuaries."

The professor shrugged. "Common Jewish names."

So far I hadn't learned anything new. But at least my talk with Professor Nevon hadn't yet devolved into a disagreement, like the conversation I'd had with Tovah at the Rockefeller Museum. I had been too eager, trying too hard to get to the center of the debate too quickly. My plan had backfired and I had learned my lesson. Best to ease into the conversation, I decided, and try to lead the conversation into the direction I wanted it to go.

"Jesus: wasn't that a name on one of the ossuaries?" I asked.

"Yes."

"And Mary. And Matthew. And...let's see..." I flipped back through several pages of notes, pretending I needed assistance remembering the other names.

"...And Joseph, Judah, and another Mary," the professor said.

"Yes, thank you." Then I laughed, as if suddenly amused by something. "Funny to imagine that a silly documentary started this whole controversy."

Writing in my notebook as I said this, I was aware of a sudden calm in the room. The professor was silent and still, and all I could hear were the buzz of the florescent lights above us and the sound of my own scribbling. I dotted an "i" and crossed a "t" and looked up from my notebook.

The professor was looking past me, just over my left shoulder, his eyes fixated as if focused on some object in the distance behind me.

"The documentary," he whispered.

"Have you seen it?"

The professor seemed to be lost in his own world; he didn't answer, just continued to stare off into space, searching for something in the distance.

"Dr. Nevon...?" I said. Nothing. "Dr. Nevon...?"

The professor finally snapped to and his eyes met mine. "My apologies..." he said, clearing his throat. "You asked about the documentary...Yes, I've seen it."

"Are you OK?" I asked, and he nodded without further explanation. So I continued, slowly. "Do you think the documentary is far-fetched? Or could there be truth to it?"

"Well, you heard what I told my students. The mystery lives on..." He paused, and it felt like he was still pulling his mind back from wherever it had just been. His responses were more scattered, less focused, with less depth. "More time and more research will tell..."

"So, then, speaking of more research..." I began, before I launched into my next question. I wanted to give him time to focus, to be fully present in the moment.

"Yes?" he said.

"Other than that documentary, has there been any photos or videos released of what the tomb looks like?"

"The IAA released a report, documenting what was found inside, with pictures of the six inscribed ossuaries. But no pictures of the tomb itself. One of the archeologists who excavated the tomb released his own report as well, with detailed sketches of the interior and exterior of the tomb. Again, no pictures."

I was scribbling in my notebook when the next question came right out of my mouth without a thought.

"Are the reports accurate with what you've seen?"

There was a pause, a silence in the air but the faint scratching sound of my pen on paper.

"What I've seen?" the professor finally said.

I cringed and stopped writing, realizing what I'd just suggested. I stared at my notebook a minute, afraid to meet his eyes. When I looked up, his eyes were darting back and forth, searching mine for an explanation.

"What do you mean, 'what I've seen'"? he repeated.

I took a couple of deep breaths, unsure how I was going to recover from my verbal faux pas. I'd been hoping he would've simply confessed to seeing the tomb and agreed to help me gain access, without having to involve Lev. Without me even having to mention Lev at all.

How presumptuous of me. How impetuous...and how stupid.

In that moment I felt way in over my head. Embarrassed and ashamed. And about to get someone I hardly knew in trouble. So I thought it best to simply go.

"I'm so sorry, professor," I said, putting my notebook and pen back into my bag and standing to leave. "I shouldn't have come. But I really appreciate your time."

Perhaps I'd find another way, I thought to myself. Or perhaps I didn't need to see the tomb at all. Maybe I should leave Jerusalem; I could do research from home.

Dr. Nevon stood. "I...I don't understand. What's going on?"

I took an extra-long and deep breath.

"Lev sent me," I said.

I wasn't sure the professor would know who Lev was, since I didn't know his last name and for all I knew the professor could've had several students named Lev over the years. Or friends named Lev. Or relatives named Lev. I could be talking about anybody. Or nobody at all.

There was a moment of silence as the professor looked at me, and then at the ground, and then at me again, before finally saying, "Oh, I see."

"Do you know who I'm talking about, professor?"

"Yes, I do," he said, smiling wistfully.

"I want to see the ossuaries—and maybe even the tomb itself. Lev thought you'd be able to help me. But now I realize how silly an idea that was."

I turned to walk away, feeling defeated and ashamed, and the professor reached out and touched my shoulder.

"Miss Beltane?"

I turned to face him again. "Please, call me Mara."

Dr. Nevon smiled. "Mara, meet me for lunch tomorrow at the café on Tiferet Yisrael Street. I want to tell you my story. And I will tell you everything I know."

CHAPTER NINE

I spent the next morning holed up in my hotel room, reviewing my notes from Dr. Nevon's class, pouring over everything I'd found on the Internet about the Talpiot tomb, and scanning books I'd brought along on the subject of the supposed lost tomb of Jesus. I was hoping the brainstorming session would help me flesh out a riveting action-filled plot for the novel I would write.

I was unsure how I should begin the novel, but I knew what I wanted the ending to be: that the Talpiot tomb was indeed the final resting place of Jesus Christ, not the Church of the Holy Sepulchre, and that the six inscribed ossuaries belonged to Jesus and various members of his family. Hence Mary Magdalene was his wife, and Judah, their son. I wasn't going to hint at the idea of a Jesus family tree, I would hopefully prove it was possible.

The professor promised to tell me everything he knew about the tomb. But why? Why was he suddenly willing to share his knowledge with me? Wasn't he worried about the possible consequences?

Hopefully I would discover all the answers in a few short hours during my lunch meeting with him. At the moment, though, I had to be patient, stay focused, and stop looking at my watch every ten minutes.

My cell phone rang, and it startled me. I retrieved it from the bed and sat back down at the desk.

"Hello?"

"Is this Mara Beltane?" a slightly accented, raspy female voice asked.

"Yes."

"This is Abigail Greenberg, biblical archeologist with Bar Ilan University. You e-mailed me about a story you were writing?"

"Oh, yes!" I said, excited that someone had finally responded to my request for interviews. I had emailed about a dozen or so scholars, academics, authors, and archeologists before leaving the States, several of them Jerusalem-based, requesting interviews. I wasn't surprised that none had responded; I hadn't been totally forthcoming about who I was or what I was writing, but I hadn't lied either.

"Remind me again what the story is about," Abigail said.

"It's not a story. I'm actually writing a novel...about the Talpiot tomb."

"A novel about the Talpiot tomb."

"I'm sorry, I only just kind of mentioned that in my email. I hope that doesn't make you not want to talk to me."

Abigail laughed. "That actually makes me want to talk to you more! The world needs a good biblical thriller about the Talpiot tomb. All the academic information that exists is so dry and boring and unsexy. Facts and figures and dates and timelines and historical names blah blah blah..."

"So you're familiar with it?"

"Oh, sure," she said. "What do you want to know?"

No sense in beating around the bush. "I'm trying to find out if it's possible that the tomb is the final resting place of Jesus Christ."

"Oy! Okay," Abigail said, laughing.

"What can you tell me about it, from your perspective?"

"I was probably thirty years-old when the tomb was discovered all those year ago," Abigail said. "I can tell you the discovery of the tomb was just that: another discovery. All discoveries are exciting, of course, but there was nothing extraordinary about this one."

"Were you involved at all with the excavation?"

"Oh, no. The IAA had full authority of the site. I wasn't even in Jerusalem at the time, anyway."

"Where were you?"

"Let's see. It was 1980, right? I think I was doing research in Qumran...No, wait. I might've been excavating in Jezreel...or maybe I was in Jericho..."

"You've been to all those places?"

"I'm a biblical archeologist, my dear! It's part of my job." Abigail laughed, a hearty, chest-rattling sound that gave her away as a smoker.

"So you probably didn't get to see the Talpiot tomb at all?" I said.

"Like I said, I'm not a member of the IAA, and my services weren't called upon. Besides, it only took the IAA two weeks to completely excavate the tomb. By the time I arrived home from wherever I was, the Talpiot tomb was long forgotten."

The Israel Antiquities Authority, or IAA for short, was responsible for the safeguarding of all of Israel's antiquities and treasures. Surely being a member of the largest archeological organization in all of Israel was an important and delicate job, a job with lots of responsibilities and authority...and power.

It gave me an idea.

"The IAA was in charge of the Talpiot tomb excavation..." I said, more to myself than to Abigail. I scribbled furiously in my notebook as I spoke.

"Yes," Abigail confirmed.

"So that means the IAA was responsible for analysis and storage of the tomb's contents as well?"

"Correct."

"Including the six inscribed ossuaries?"

"Of course."

"And those six ossuaries were catalogued and put away for safe keeping in a storage facility, never to see the light of day. And the tomb, as you said, was excavated very quickly and soon forgotten."

Abigail laughed. "What are you getting at, my dear? Some kind of cover-up?"

"Well, sure. A cover-up, or a conspiracy..."

"Conspiracy..."

"Sure. By a government agency that wields a lot of power. Perhaps too much power..."

Abigail was silent a moment. Finally, she said, "Sounds like a good plot for a novel."

In that moment I was having a breakthrough. Another piece of my novel's puzzle had fallen into place. I now had my antagonist, my bad guy, the person, or people, who would stop at nothing to keep the Talpiot tomb's secrets hidden forever.

"The IAA is involved in all matters concerning Israel's antiquities," Abigail was saying as I returned my focus to our conversation. "That's its job. So of course the IAA was involved with all aspects of the Talpiot tomb excavation and the safe-keeping of its contents. I hope you don't think I was insinuating anything beyond that."

"Of course not," I said. "But don't you think it's strange that a lot of the IAA's discoveries are on display at the Israel and Rockefeller Museums, but the six inscribed ossuaries from the Talpiot tomb are hidden away in a storeroom miles from there?"

"Are you asking for my personal opinion?"

"Yes. Because as you can imagine, having some evidence of the Talpiot tomb being the final resting place of Jesus goes a long way in making my book more believable, even if it is, you know, fiction."

Abigail paused before answering.

"Are you a religious woman, Miss Beltane?" she asked.

"Please, call me Mara," I said. "And no, I'm not religious."

"Well, you asked me for my personal opinion. Here it is. Everybody answers to somebody...or something. Most scientists, for example, are not interested in beliefs and theories. We need hard evidence—absolute, undeniable proof—in order to believe. In other words, we answer to science. But men and women of faith, the truly devout...well, it doesn't matter what evidence you present. And historical accuracy is not important to them. They answer only to God."

Abigail was absolutely right. My father was a prime example. He went to church every week and prayed to God and praised Jesus despite the lack of scientific evidence proving they existed. Because other than the Bible, what evidence is there? What would it take for my father to suddenly not believe? What would cause him to turn his back on religion? A stone box with Jesus' name on it?

I didn't think so.

Religious belief, to me, is so deep-seated as to defy all logic and reasoning and scientific evidence. It is, I believe, beyond proof or disproof.

"Tomb or no tomb," Abigail continued, "followers of Jesus simply trust he is the true Son of God. And they are more than willing to fight for this belief. Keep this in mind as you set out to prove if the Talpiot tomb is the final resting place of Jesus."

"You're interested in biblical history," I said. "As a historian and archeologist, aren't you the least bit curious?"

"My time has come and gone," Abigail said, sighing. "I will be retiring soon, clearing the way for someone else to discover more about the history of our world. Perhaps that person will discover the truth about the Talpiot tomb."

"Maybe someone like Dr. Uri Nevon," I said softly to myself. But I had spoken louder than I thought.

"Ah, yes. My dear friend Uri," Abigail said. "If anyone can convince the world the Talpiot tomb is real, it's him. If he took up the cause, that is."

"How do you know him?"

"I was a guest lecturer at Bar Ilan University when he was an undergraduate student there. Oh, that must be twenty years ago now. That is when we first met."

"And you stayed in touch with him?"

"From time to time. He'd contact me whenever he had archeology questions. Do you know him?"

"We actually met yesterday. I sought him out because...well, I heard through the grapevine that he knew a lot about the Talpiot tomb."

"He's done a lot of...research...shall we say," Abigail said. "Did he happen to mention that?"

"Not exactly, but I got the sense that he knows more than he's letting on."

"We spoke a lot when he was researching the Talpiot tomb. That was somewhat recently."

I took a deep breath, and then I took a gamble. "I think he illegally gained access to the tomb."

"Do you think, or do you know?"

"Right now it's just a hunch. But by tomorrow I'm hoping to know for sure. We're meeting for lunch. He claims he's going to tell me what he knows."

"Well, then," Abigail said. "Here's what *I* know, and this piece of information doesn't need to make it back to him..."

"Of course not," I promised. "I'd never betray your confidence."

"He asked for my blessing before he did it."

I inhaled sharply, my suspicion confirmed.

"What did you say?" I asked. "What did you do?"

"What could I do?" she said. "He had his heart set on it."

"You didn't try to stop him?"

"My dear, you do not know the professor the way I do. But spend some time with him and you'll discover there's no stopping him once an idea takes hold."

"I'm lucky I found him at all. It was quite by accident, actually."

"Accident?" Abigail said. "I'd say more like *bashert*."

"Bashert?"

Abigail explained that *bashert* was the Yiddish word for fate.

"Perhaps it was your destiny to meet Uri," she said. "Fate, for whatever reason, brought you two together. You're looking for answers about the Talpiot tomb, and he knows more about it than anyone."

Looking back, I certainly believe fate played a hand in our meeting. And in more ways than Abigail, or I, could've ever imagined at the time.

"Uri must have a good feeling about you," Abigail said. "I know I do. Which is why I felt comfortable confirming your suspicion, which is not a betrayal of friendship, as far as I'm concerned. The rest of the details? Well, that's up to him."

Abigail and I wrapped up our conversation. Her last words to me were equal parts warning and blessing.

"May God watch over you, my dear. You will need it for this adventure you are about to undertake."

CHAPTER TEN

I walked through the streets of Old City feeling that Dr. Uri Nevon was the key to helping me bust this case wide open. I had already been cautioned by Abigail and scoffed at by Tovah in my attempts to learn about any secrets the Talpiot tomb may be hiding. So I felt there was a deeper mystery at play. And the professor would hopefully guide me and provide some answers.

What I ultimately wanted to do—what I felt I *needed* to do—was see the tomb for myself. But gaining access was illegal. Would the professor be willing to break the law to help me? Maybe his supposed obsession with the Talpiot tomb was enough of an incentive. I sure hoped so, because the future of my book depended on it. And it was too early in the process to let the idea for my next novel slip through my fingers...

So, while there was self-imposed pressure to nurture a novel idea, getting to know Jerusalem and its people was a substantial help.

Most of the trips I'd taken with Thomas required hustling from one city to another. Sometimes we barely had a chance to stop and listen to life happening around us, to truly experience the places and its people. We had traveled to nearly twenty countries, but had we really "seen" any of them?

This trip was different. There was no need to hurry. Although I lived with a constant sense of urgency, I allowed myself time to research, as long as it took. And to do that, I had to completely immerse myself in the culture of Jerusalem.

It helped that I was seeing the same faces every day: hotel staff, bartenders, restaurant wait staff, market vendors. They smiled and waved at me, and sometimes called my name as I passed. I was starting to know my way around, and could find places without the aid of a map. This knowledge allowed me to walk the streets of Old City and New City with confidence, as if I was a local, like I fit in, like I belonged.

So even if the book didn't pan out or it wound up being a failure, I would consider the trip a success because I felt I at least had conquered a foreign city all by myself. I had that to be proud of.

I turned onto Tiferet Yisrael Street, one of the busiest streets in the Jewish Quarter. It connects the tree-shaded Hurva Square with the stairs that descend to the Western Wall. Once past the Hurva Square and near the end of the street I would find the café where Professor Nevon had instructed me to meet him for lunch.

The café was small and simple, with a few tables outside for alfresco dining, a popular pastime in Jerusalem. I had passed the café several times during my walks through the Old City and thought nothing of it. But it must have some significance if he requested this specific site for us to meet.

The professor was sitting at a table outside the café, sipping a beer and reading a newspaper. He was wearing khaki pants and a light green button-down shirt with the sleeves rolled up to his elbows. I felt slightly underdressed in my tan slacks, red short-sleeved shirt and hiking boots. He looked up as I approached, folded his paper and rose to greet me.

"Out walking again?" he asked.

I was surprised that he remembered this little detail of our conversation the previous day in which I told him walking was my favorite way to get to know a city. I smiled and replied that his city was very walkable.

We both sat and a waitress came over and handed each of us a menu. She said something to me in Hebrew, and I looked at Dr. Nevon, wide-eyed and embarrassed. He said something to her, and she rested her gaze on me and smiled.

"Would you like something to drink?" she said in perfect English.

The menu was mostly in Hebrew, but I was able to decipher the word Coke among the choices of available beverages. "Coke, please," I said.

"I recommend a falafel," the professor said to me. "They're very good here."

"Okay, Coke and a falafel," I told the waitress, and the professor ordered a falafel for himself.

"So, Mara, how long have you been in Jerusalem?" he asked once the waitress had taken her leave.

"A few days."

"Are you enjoying it so far?"

"Very much. It's a beautiful city. I hope to make the most of my time here."

"And you're here to learn about the Talpiot tomb? Write a novel about it?"

"Yes."

"There are....some things I can tell you," he said.

I reached into my bag and pulled out my notebook and a pen, asking the professor if he minded that I take notes. He said he didn't mind. When I glanced up, he was looking at me in that curious way of his, his eyebrows raised and mouth set, the way I had seen him address his students. I supposed he was waiting for me to start asking questions.

"Well, Dr. Nevon, I—"

"Please," the professor interjected. "Call me Uri."

The waitress appeared and placed a glass of Coke in front of me, as well as a straw. I thanked her and she walked away with a brisk "you're welcome."

"The documentary I mentioned to you in class yesterday is what brought me here," I said. "It's what inspired the idea for the novel I want to write."

"I see," Uri said, smiling. "First and foremost, the documentary suggests there's a Jesus family tree."

"Yes, that is very interesting. So maybe we can start there? By discussing his family? The ossuaries found in the tomb were supposedly family members."

Uri took a swig of beer and allowed me to continue.

"Mary Magdalene, for example. There was an ossuary found in the Talpiot tomb that supposedly had an inscription with her name on it."

"Ah, yes," Uri said, taking another sip of beer. "Mariamene e Mara. Perhaps the most controversial of the ossuaries."

"That was the inscription on the bone box."

"Yes. Mariamene is a Greek form of Mary, and Mara is an Aramaic word meaning *master*." Uri sat forward and leaned across the table. "Did your parents know that when they named you?"

"I—I don't know," I said, suddenly recalling the origin of the word Mara. I didn't think my parents would be familiar with Aramaic, a dead language. So perhaps they had simply heard the name somewhere and liked it enough to give it to their only child.

"Well, in any case," Uri continued, "the fact remains that if this is indeed the ossuary of Mary Magdalene, and we are to believe the inscription translates as *Mary the master,* then we must accept that the inscription was written in two different languages, Greek and Aramaic."

"Is that possible?" I asked, writing in my notebook.

"It's very rare. None of the other ossuaries found in antiquity—about two thousand—either mix languages or give a title to a person, such as *master*. Therefore, we must present another possibility."

"Which is?" I asked, taking a long sip from the straw and continuing to take notes as Uri spoke.

"That the inscription is written in a single language, in this case Greek, a common language at the time and the more common way to inscribe bone boxes. If you then translate the bone box inscription into strictly Greek, it becomes *Mariamene and Mara*. Mariamene again being a form of Mary, and Mara, in this case, being a form of Martha."

As I scribbled these revelations furiously, the weight of his last statement sank in.

"So you're saying there could have been *two* women buried in the same bone box?"

"It's possible," Uri said. "We know that the first name, Mariamene, was written in formal Greek script. It's possible that the second name, Mara, translated as Martha, was written in a different cursive Greek script—not Aramaic. This could suggest that the bones of a second woman were added later to the ossuary, and a different scribe wrote the name of the second woman on the box."

"So the box contains the bones of two women, interred at separate times," I summarized.

"That's one theory." Uri took another sip of beer and I took another long sip of my Coke, thirsty from the heat.

"Was it common to have multiple people buried in the same ossuary?" I asked.

"There are reports of family tombs with ossuaries containing up to six people. In Judaism, you can be buried with whomever you slept with in the same bed. A husband and wife being the most obvious example. But also siblings or family members who grew up together. Or a mother who shared her bed with her young children."

The waitress brought our falafels and I waited for her to turn away before continuing.

"If you take the two-women-in-one-ossuary theory into account, then the house of cards falls apart," I said. "The ossuary can't possibly be that of Mary Magdalene, and therefore the Talpiot tomb can't be the tomb of Jesus Christ."

Uri took a bite of falafel and chased it with a sip of beer. "Unless," he said, "you consider another Jewish law: unrelated women were not allowed to be buried together. Mariamene and Mara, therefore, could have been, say, sisters. Who's to say Mariamene didn't refer to Mary Magdalene, and that she had a sister, Mara? If that's the case, then it makes sense that they were both buried with Jesus. Because Mariamene, or Mary Magdalene, was married to him. Or so the documentary claims."

My head was spinning from the combination of heat and complicated conversation. I leaned back in my chair and rubbed my right temple.

"Okay, so it seems to me that the validity of the Talpiot tomb rests with the Mariamene e Mara ossuary," I said. "If you remove it from the equation, what you're left with is a tomb filled with ossuaries belonging to a typical extended Jewish family whose names were very common for the period."

"Yes, that's true," Uri said. "But to say that the names were common is a shallow argument. It's the *cluster* of names—Mary, Jesus, Joseph, and so on—that is uncommon and rare."

Without realizing it, I had finished my entire falafel and all but a few sips of Coke. Both my head and my stomach were full. Uri's plate was empty as well, and he'd just taken his last swig of beer. I only had one question left in me.

"Do you believe the Talpiot tomb is the final resting place of Jesus Christ?" I asked.

Uri smiled, then paused. "What do you think of this café?" he asked.

"Oh...uh, well, it's very nice. The food is delicious. Thank you for suggesting it."

"I'm glad you like it. It's one of my favorite places, but not just for the food." Uri motioned to his left, to a hill that rose to the east of Old City. He was pointing to the Mount of Olives.

The Mount of Olives had been used as a burial ground since the third millennium B.C. More importantly, this area of Jerusalem was associated with the last days of Jesus. It was the area I was headed to on the day I met Lev, but I never made it.

"That is where my people are buried," Uri said, continuing to point. "They have been resting there for centuries. And it's the place where I, too, will be buried one day."

As I stared up at the mountain, dotted with churches and Jewish graves, I marveled at how spectacular the Old City, and New City beyond, must look from up there.

"I never tire of this view," Uri said. "Have you visited the Mount of Olives yet?"

I returned my gaze to Uri. As I stared at his profile and admired his handsome features, I realized the professor was not going to answer my question. He wasn't ready to reveal himself.

"No, I haven't," I said. "But I've been meaning to..."

"Excellent," he said, looking me deep in the eyes. "You must allow me to take you there."

CHAPTER ELEVEN

We stood atop the Mount of Olives, the walls of the Old City down to our right, and the Valley of Jehoshaphat below us. Rows of sand-colored stone tombs spread out in front of us, numbering in the thousands, evidence that millennia of Jews believed this to be the place where the dead would be resurrected on the Day of Judgment. Christians and Muslims hold this same belief, so the valley is dotted with the cemeteries of three major faiths.

Yesterday I sat at the outdoor café with Uri, looking up at the Mount of Olives from within the walls of the Old City, and wondered how spectacular the view must be from up there. Now I knew. From atop the Mount of Olives, just outside the Mosque of the Ascension where I stood with Uri at my side, I could see it all: the whole Kidron Valley, or Valley of Jehoshaphat; Mount Zion across the valley, the hill synonymous with biblical times and the final days of Jesus; and the Dome of the Rock off in the distance, its gold dome a shining beacon proclaiming the glory of Jerusalem.

Uri broke the silence that had existed between us for several minutes as I took in the vastness and grandeur of Jerusalem.

"Would you believe that after the birth of Israel, a time that was supposed to be happy and prosperous, the Palestinians desecrated our sacred sites and destroyed much of Jerusalem," he said. He pointed down to the Jewish cemeteries below us in the Valley of Jehoshaphat. "During the years of Palestinian occupation, many tombstones just like those were used as paving stones for roads. Many of the cemeteries were converted into parking lots."

"How awful," I said.

"The birth of Israel was a violent one," he continued. "Especially in Jerusalem. Jerusalem has always been the heart of the conflict. If you are to know Jerusalem, this is the first thing you must understand."

"Do you remember much of the conflict?" I asked, trying to discern how old Uri was.

"My parents lived during the British Mandate, a time of relative peace in Israel and in Jerusalem. There was not a lot of violence, but not much happened in the way of making Israel its own governing state. After the birth of Israel, my family survived many years of war and occupation by various Arab nations wanting to proclaim Jerusalem as their own. Many friends and family members were forced from their land; some were killed. Still others emigrated to America."

"Did your parents stay?" I asked.

"They refused to leave. Jerusalem was their home. They are resting now, down there." Uri pointed to the dozens of rows of tombs below us.

Uri paused, his eyes again scanning the landscape.

"By the time I was born the War of 1967 had just ended and Israel had regained control of the West Bank and East Jerusalem."

"Things didn't stay peaceful for long, though…" I said.

"No, they did not. Israel would not give up any land it had captured during the War of 1967 in exchange for peace talks. In fact, Israel tried to expand its territorial reach even further by building settlements on the West Bank of the Jordan River, land the Palestinians claim is theirs."

"Settlements are still being built today," I added. "This is illegal, I think?"

"It depends on who you ask. The Geneva Convention may say it is illegal, but Jews are the people of the Bible." Uri held a hand to his chest. "We believe we are doing God's work. The Old Testament promised us this land."

"And the Palestinians?" I asked. "What do they think of all this?"

"They think we are thieves," he said, a tone of resentment in his voice. "They think we are stealing land that belongs to them."

"Why do they think this land belongs to them?"

"Their claims of territory ownership are based on centuries of occupation."

"So the Jewish viewpoint is based on an ancient pact with God, while the Arab viewpoint is based on who's lived in the Holy Land longer?"

"It is more complicated than that, of course," Uri said. "But you have cut to the heart of it."

"And future generations? What do you think they'll face?"

Uri sighed. "If I had children, I would fear for their future. I am optimistic that we'll see an end to the conflict, but I don't think it'll be in my lifetime."

Until then, it didn't occur to me that Uri could've had children. He wore no wedding ring and never spoke of a wife. Being childless myself, I didn't think to ask if he had any children of his own. I thought of Uri as simply a man and a professor—not as a man, professor, husband, and father.

Uri wasn't a father, but was he a husband or boyfriend?

"So, who's right?" I asked, pushing the thought of Uri's relationship status from my mind.

"I have Arab friends," Uri said. "I respect them and their religion. I don't think it is a matter of right or wrong."

Then he spun around, his arms in the air. "Look around you!" he said. "Have you seen a site more beautiful?"

Uri had refused, yet again, to answer a delicate question, to give his opinion on a sensitive subject. Perhaps the professor in him forbade him from tainting the education of others with his own ideologies.

"Jerusalem is a troubled yet culturally rich city," I said. "I can see why you want to stay here and be buried near your ancestors."

Uri nodded, then motioned me inside the Mosque of the Ascension. "Now, come inside," he said. "There is something you must see."

• • • •

MY LACK OF RELIGION meant I didn't see the insides of many churches as a child. I saw two, to be exact. But once I got married and started traveling the world with Thomas, churches were almost always on the top of my list of things to see. Not from a religious standpoint, from a cultural and architectural standpoint. Churches always wound up being the most beautiful and historic buildings in a city.

But this troubled me. Here were these churches, these cathedrals—grandiose, ostentatious, expensive monuments—lorded over by men who preached piety and selflessness and simple living. How hypocritical. Because in reality, these men of God dressed up every Sunday in their costly silken robes and prayed in their gilded, gold-laced temples in search of redemption.

They are human, after all, tempted by the same sins as the rest of us—cheating, stealing, lying, abusing. And they were searching inside their temples for a clean slate. They hoped the beauty of it all would save their sinful souls.

It was fear that kept them praying. Fear of what might happen to them if they died before atoning for their sins. Catholicism, in fact, was invented to keep people living in fear. I was sure of it.

Jesus was invented, too. He's merely a fictional character. His life was fabricated. Every story in the Bible was just that: a story. And these stories were created to stand as a lesson for us all. Never do bad things; only ever do good things. And if you find yourself committing a bad act, atone for it. Otherwise, you'll never go to heaven.

All these stories were then compiled into a book called the Bible. It was sold to the masses as the truth, a way to emotionally manipulate millions of people into believing that if you were a sinner, life after death meant eternity in hell.

And the Catholic Church got rich, gained power, and its coffers swelled...

Meanwhile, millions of people all over the world were scared straight. And as long as people were scared, they'd continue to go to church and pray, and they'd continue to hand over their hard-earned money to an establishment that did nothing but lie to them.

At least, that's what I believed as a teenager. My views of religion have softened over the years—from believing that organized religion is fundamentally flawed and corrupt to accepting that religion is a powerful thing that must be respected, if not completely understood. Still, to this day, when people ask me the best novel I ever read, I say the Bible.

And now here I was, stepping inside a religious temple for the first time in awhile, with a man whose own faith was completely foreign to me. So in spite of my lack of religion, I said a little prayer on my way in—asking that I wouldn't say or do anything to offend my new Jewish friend.

"Mara, look. Over here," Uri said, directing me to the other side of the stone interior of the Mosque of the Ascension. He pointed down to four elongated slabs of rock that formed a rectangle around what appeared to be a footprint set in stone.

Uri explained the history of the building, how it was originally built as a chapel in the fourth century A.D. to commemorate Christ's ascension. Over the centuries it was added to and rebuilt, until finally it became a Muslim shrine in the 12th century.

"Centuries ago, many believed a miracle occurred in this building," Uri said. "Dust from the floor formed the image of Christ's footprints. Eventually they were set in stone, but by then only the right foot remained."

I crouched down so I could get a better look at the supposed right footprint of Jesus Christ. It didn't look like much to me, but I allowed myself to imagine what it must've been like for early Christians to see such a thing. To them, believers of a new and burgeoning religion, knowing they walked where Jesus walked, it could have been no other person but him who left his mark in the dust.

From there, Uri showed me the Church of the Paternoster, built above a grotto where Christ supposedly taught the Lord's prayer; down a dirt path surrounded by densely-packed Jewish cemeteries; and over to the Dominus Flevit Chapel, the site where medieval pilgrims believed Jesus sat on a rock and wept over the fate of Jerusalem. We paused briefly at the chapel's west window to gaze out at the breathtaking view of Old City, framed perfectly by the Dome of the Rock at the center.

By the time we'd descended to the bottom of the Mount of Olives several hours later and stood in the Garden of Gethsemane, the site of Christ's betrayal by Judas, I was delirious from the heat, dizzy from the whirlwind tour, and in desperate need of rest.

I looked around for someplace to sit, my face flushed and my body unsteady.

"Only a little bit further to Mount Zion," Uri promised, encouraging me forward. "No tour is complete without seeing the hill synonymous with the Holy Land."

• • • •

AFTER A BREAK FOR lunch, Uri took me to St. Peter in Gallicantu, the church commemorating the traditional site of St. Peter's denial of Christ. He took me down to the crypt, where a series of caves are said to be the place Jesus spent the night before being taken to Pontius Pilate. I welcomed the respite from the desert heat, where even a damp, dark cave offered relief.

Uri did not let me pause long, however, because there was much more he wanted me to see: The Church of the Dormition, where the Virgin Mary is said to have fallen into "eternal slumber"; the Hall of the Last Supper, on the first floor of a Gothic building, said to be the site of Christ's last meal with his Disciples; and beneath the Hall of the Last Supper, King David's tomb, one of the most revered Jewish holy sites.

According to tradition, King David's tomb is also the site where Christ washed the feet of his Disciples after the Last Supper.

By the time we'd climbed down to this underground holy site, I could go no further. My feet ached, my head was spinning, and my stomach was growling again for nourishment. I collapsed on a rock inside the main chamber to rest momentarily, before Uri would no doubt whisk me to some other place—a tomb, a chapel, a grotto, a cemetery.

In the low light of the cave, there was intense quiet. Occasionally my heart fluttered as it settled down to a normal rhythm. Suddenly I heard an unusual noise in the room, like labored breaths echoing in a hollow tunnel. The sounds seemed to originate from right next to me, as if they were meant for my ears only. Why did the noises sound familiar? Where had I heard them before?

It took several seconds for me to make the connection. This morning, while I was in my hotel room preparing for my day trip with Uri, my cell phone rang. I said hello several times but whoever was on the other end refused to speak. But someone was on the other end because I heard them breathing. Labored, echoed breaths, as if the caller was running through a tunnel.

Startled, I rose from my rock perch and peeked my head around the corners into the adjoining rooms to look for other visitors. There was no one, the rooms were empty.

"Did you hear that?" I asked Uri, returning to the rock where I'd just sat.

"No," he said, looking at me curiously.

"I must be imagining things. The heat and exhaustion are playing tricks on my mind."

"What did you hear?"

"It sounded like...someone breathing."

"Breathing?" Uri asked.

"It could have come from anywhere, but it sounded like someone was standing right next to me, breathing in my left ear."

Uri took a step closer and listened for a moment. He shook his head. "No, I'm sorry," he said. "I heard nothing."

"I got a call this morning on my cell phone, and the person on the other end was breathing heavily but didn't say anything," I explained to Uri. "The noise I heard a minute ago sounded just like that. I think I'm going crazy." I don't know what made me connect the two, or why I felt the need to tell Uri, but it just came out of my mouth without thought.

"What?" Uri said, facing me directly now, a look of concern on his face.

"I said I think I'm going crazy."

"Yes, I understood that part. You said you got a call on your cell phone this morning?"

In the low light I could see his eyes darting back and forth as he searched my face for answers. He was standing close to me, and now I could hear his breathing as well as my own.

"I could hear someone on the other end but they didn't say anything," I said. "They eventually hung up. It must have been a prank call, or maybe someone accidentally dialed the wrong number..."

Uri placed his hands gently on my shoulders. "What time did you receive that phone call?"

"It was right before I met you. So, around 9 a.m."

"Not again," Uri said, sighing. "Not you, too." He looked up at the low ceiling of the cave, shaking his head.

"I don't understand," I said. "What do you mean?"

In that moment, in the cramped confines of a dim cave, I felt myself starting to succumb: my body, to the intense weight of sheer exhaustion; my brain, to the deranged hallucination of a disembodied voice; my heart, to the gentle touch of a beautiful stranger.

"So you want to see the Talpiot tomb?" he asked.

"Yes, of course. It's my whole reason for being here."

"Then we must hurry before it's too late."

"Too late for what?"

Uri waved off my question. "Meet me tomorrow morning at Lev's shop. If you want to see the Talpiot tomb, then it must be soon."

"Why the sudden hurry?"

"Talk to Lev," Uri said, holding up a hand to stave off further questions. "He has the answers. And he is the only one who can get us inside."

CHAPTER TWELVE

"**H**ello again, Miss Mara," the boy said to me, smiling. He was arranging items on one of the glass display cases in the middle of his small store when I returned, a day after visiting the Mount of Olives with Uri.

"Hello, Lev," I said.

"What brings you back to my store? Looking for another olive wood trinket?" He pushed his glasses further up on his nose.

When we'd met for the first time several days before, Lev wore jeans and a pull-over collared shirt, a casual look that almost pegged him as a traveler, not a proprietor-in-training. Today, however, he fit the bill, wearing a white dress shirt tucked into a pair of dark blue slacks.

"Well, I—" I started.

Just then the chime above the door sounded. Lev turned towards the door to see who had entered and was surprised to see Uri standing in the threshold. His mouth fell in shock.

"Professor Nevon," he said, quickly replacing the items he held back on the shelf. "What are you doing here?"

"It's nice to see you, too, Lev," Uri said, laughing.

"I'm sorry," Lev said. "Where are my manners? How have you been?" He walked closer to where Uri and I stood.

"I've been well." Uri looked around the store, at the white walls painted with intricate patterns in blue and green, at the service counter in the back of the room, and finally to the glass display cases in the middle of the store near where Lev stood. The two men's eyes met once again.

"I like what you've done with the store," Uri said. "You've painted since I've seen it last."

"Yes," Lev said. "It was long overdue."

There was a moment of silence before Uri finally said, "It has been too long, my old friend."

Lev looked uneasy. His eyes darted between me and Uri. "So...what brings you both here?"

"Lev, I'm sorry," I said, feeling the need to apologize for our unexpected visit. "I want you to know that—"

"Mara, it's okay," Uri said, placing a hand on my shoulder. "Let me explain."

Lev's shoulders hunched slightly and he glared at Uri. "You want my help getting inside the Talpiot tomb, don't you?" He slid his accusing eyes to me. "That's why you're both here."

"Yes," Uri confirmed.

"Professor, I referred Miss Mara to you because I thought you would help her," Lev said, clearly agitated. "Please don't involve me! I got in so much trouble last time!"

Uri stepped forward and reached his hand out, as if to comfort Lev with a friendly squeeze on the arm. "I know, Lev. I understand. Just listen..."

"You don't need my help," Lev said, shrugging away from Uri's touch.

"Yes, we do," Uri said. "You are the only one with influence."

"Professor, I have shamed my family! And I have police watching my every move!"

All I could do was stand there in stunned silence as the two Israelis carried on with their own private conversation.

"We were foolish last time," Uri said. "We won't be this time. We'll better prepare, have a back-up plan."

Lev threw his hands in the air. "Hasn't this tomb cost you enough?"

Uri lowered his head, as if to give himself a private moment to think. He sighed, then looked at Lev. "I don't regret what we did. Do you?"

"I...I don't know," Lev said.

"Wasn't it worth it in the end, to see what only a handful of people in the whole world have seen?" Uri said. "To experience what may be the most significant find of all antiquity?"

Lev did not respond. His eyes were skyward, searching, like the appropriate reply was written on the ceiling.

Uri tried again to get through to the boy. "Was your sacrifice too great?"

Lev sighed and flopped his long arms against his sides in what looked like a sign of defeat.

"I feel sorry for you, professor, really I do," he said. "Your sacrifice was much greater than mine, of course. But that was your choice, not mine. You came to me. You asked for my help."

"I do not blame you for what happened to me, Lev. You are right. I asked for your help and you gave it, willingly and unselfishly. Believe me, I feel guilty for what happened to you."

"Then why?" Lev asked. "Why ask me to sacrifice again? Why take the risk when we all have so much to lose?"

"Look at this opportunity we have been given," Uri said, grasping his hands together as if imploring, almost begging, Lev for help. "A second chance to see the Talpiot tomb! And a chance for me to make things up to you."

"And Miss Mara?" Lev asked, acknowledging me for the first time in several minutes. "What role does she play in all this? Are you using her as your excuse to clean your slate?"

Uri shrank back, surprised by Lev's accusation. "Absolutely not!" He turned to me. "Mara, you have been given this wonderful opportunity as well. You have met two people in Jerusalem who are able to get you inside the Talpiot tomb! Isn't this what you came here for?" He raised his eyebrows and set his mouth, the way I had seen him address his students. He was waiting for me to tell him yes, that I believed his intentions were good.

My presence in Jerusalem did seem convenient for Uri. He could be using me and my desire to see the tomb for his own selfish motivations. But wasn't that the exact thing I was doing? Was I not using Lev and his connections, whatever they were, and Uri and his knowledge to write a novel that I hoped would turn Christianity on its head? Wasn't I being selfish and disingenuous?

Giving Uri and Lev a chance to see the tomb a second time did seem like a good way for me to cleanse my conscience, though. And Uri had spent a lot of time with me already, teaching me what he knew and showing me around his great city. So for those two reasons I chose to believe him.

I nodded at Uri, who smiled in recognition of my trust in him and my willingness to sacrifice whatever it took to see the Talpiot tomb. We both looked at Lev, putting the ball in his court.

Lev sighed heavily. "Fine, I'll do it," he said. He looked past the two of us and through the glass door of the shop into the bustling alleyways of the marketplace, searching. "But we can't meet here. It's too dangerous."

"It's already too late," Uri said. "Mara received a phone call yesterday. And so did I."

I snapped my head over in Uri's direction. "You received a similar call yesterday?" I asked him. "Someone breathing on the other end who didn't say anything?"

Uri nodded.

"It wasn't a prank call?" I asked.

"I'm afraid not."

"How do you know?"

"It happened last time."

"Oh. Well, what does it mean?"

"It means that someone knows what you plan to do. And they know that I am involved."

Lev's eyes grew big as he looked at us. "Miss Mara, who knows you are here in Jerusalem?"

That was an easy one. I'd only told two people. "My best friend back home in the States and my literary agent."

"Who else?" he prodded. "Who here in Jerusalem have you spoken to?"

"Abigail Greenberg," I said, looking at Uri for reassurance that the archaeologist I had spoken to several days before was who she claimed to be.

"Who?" Lev asked.

Uri smiled as if recalling an old memory. "Abigail Greenberg. She is a dear friend of mine. She taught me a lot about archeology and encouraged my studies."

Lev opened his mouth as if to object or argue but Uri cut him off.

"She poses no threat to us," Uri said.

"How do you know?" Lev asked.

"I just do."

Lev seemed to accept Uri's explanation.

"So who else knows you're here, Miss Mara? You must have spoken to someone about the Talpiot tomb...?"

The only other person I had spoken to about the Talpiot tomb was Tovah from the Rockefeller Museum. We had gotten into a rather heated discussion about the possibility of it being the final resting place of Jesus of Nazareth. As an employee of the Israel Antiquities Authority, the governing body that runs Jerusalem's museums and oversees its treasures, Tovah was probably obligated to say that the tomb and the ossuaries found inside were not extraordinary and warranted no further research. In response, I told her that it wasn't up to the IAA to decide. The tomb should be open to the public and the ossuaries should be on display, not hidden away in a warehouse. Let the court of public opinion decide.

"I think the IAA knows," I said.

"*What*?" Lev exclaimed.

Uri put up a hand to calm him. "What do you mean? How could the IAA know?"

"I had a private tour of the Rockefeller Museum a few days ago," I explained. "Which is run by the IAA, right?"

Both men nodded.

"Which makes the tour guide a member of IAA. So I asked her about the IAA's opinion, and her own personal opinion, about the Talpiot tomb and the ossuaries."

"Miss Mara! Why would you do that?" Lev asked.

"The IAA was in charge of the excavation and still stores the ossuaries in one of their facilities, so who better to ask?" I asked.

"What happened?" Uri asked me.

"Our discussion got rather heated," I said, laughing, recalling how the tour guide's nostrils flared like a bull at the mere mention of the tomb. "I mentioned the documentary that claims the tomb might belong to Jesus and his family. She denied this possibility."

"Who was your tour guide?" Uri asked.

"Tovah."

"Tovah, of course," Uri said.

"Do you know her?"

"Yes, we run in the same social circle. You have to be careful with her. She is known to be a bit of a gossip."

"Great," Lev said.

"You think she told someone about our conversation, about my interest in the tomb?" I asked Uri.

"There's a good chance." Uri stroked his chin, as if contemplating how to proceed in light of this new information. "We'll have to be especially careful now."

"I'm sorry," I said to both of them. "I didn't know. Is it really that big of a deal that Tovah knows? I mean, who could she have possibly told?"

"It could be a big deal," Lev said.

"I'd read about the IAA's response to the documentary's claims," I said. "I know that they feel the Talpiot tomb is just that: a tomb, but..."

Uri and Lev were looking at each other as I spoke.

"What?" I asked the both of them.

"Ziva," Lev said to Uri, ignoring my comment.

Uri contemplated for a moment, then nodded. "Yes, Ziva."

Again, the two Israelis ignored me and engaged in their own private conversation.

"Do you think Tovah told Ziva?" Lev asked Uri.

"It's a good possibility. Have you spoken to her much since the incident?"

"A few times," Lev said. "You?"

"Yes, a few times," Uri said. "But we mustn't worry ourselves about that right now."

Uri turned to me, determination in his eyes. "Mara, are you ready for a once-in-a-lifetime experience?"

I looked at Lev, who appeared nervous and excited at the same time.

"I suppose," I said, turning back to Uri.

"There must be certainty," Uri said. "Because once we start, there's no turning back."

CHAPTER THIRTEEN

*erusalem Post
    October 15, 2007
PROMINENT PROFESSOR, LOCAL BOY ACCUSED OF
BREAK-IN AT TALPIOT TOMB*

Dr. Uri Nevon, professor and biblical scholar at Hebrew University, and Lev Geller, a shop clerk in Old City, were arrested yesterday for illegally gaining entrance to the Talpiot tomb, a controversial burial cave in the Talpiot suburb of Jerusalem that a recent documentary claims in the lost tomb of Jesus of Nazareth.

"I heard what sounded like a jackhammer," said a resident of the apartment complex that sits beside the now-covered tomb. "I looked out my window and saw shadows and heard voices and thought something suspicious might be going on."

When police arrived on the scene, they discovered that the slab of concrete covering the tomb had been pried away. A young man, identified later as twenty-year-old Lev Geller, was found at the scene near the entrance of the tomb. He initially told police he was alone, but several minutes later the forty-year-old professor emerged from the tomb, confessing his role in the break-in. Neither men resisted arrest.

The Talpiot tomb was discovered in 1980 during a construction project. The tomb was found to contain ten ossuaries, six with names inscribed on them. The cave didn't create any controversy when it was initially found; many such tombs have been discovered in and around Jerusalem and Israel, most of which are believed to be first-century burial chambers of upper-class Jewish families.

But a recent documentary, which initially aired in early 2007, has stirred up controversy for its claim that the tomb is the final resting place of Jesus of Nazareth. The documentary also claims the cave contained the remains of several of Jesus' family members, including his mother, Mary, and brother, James, and that Jesus was married to Mary Magdalene and they had a son, Judah. The Mary Magdalene and Judah ossuaries were also found in the cave, according to the documentary.

Biblical scholars, archaeologists, and educators the world over have come forward to express their doubts and question the validity of the research that was used to derive at the claims made in the documentary. It has sparked a worldwide debate that is unlikely to end anytime soon.

It is believed Dr. Nevon gained access to the inner chamber of the tomb where the ossuaries had once been housed and was inside for several minutes before police arrived. It is also believed Mr. Geller served as a look-out. Nothing was missing from the tomb, as it had been emptied of its contents by archaeologists working for the Israel Antiquities Authority (IAA) when it was excavated 27 years ago. It is uncertain as to why the two men would want to gain access to an empty tomb.

Since the break-in, the tomb entrance has been under 24/7 surveillance.

Public speculation suggests that Dr. Nevon and Mr. Geller did not act alone, and that other parties may have been involved in helping the two men gain access to the tomb. Jerusalem police doubt this is the case.

"There is no evidence that this was an inside job, or that other parties were involved," said Jerusalem station chief Benjamin Schwarz. "There two men acted alone."

The Talpiot apartment owner's association, which arranged to have the tomb sealed after it was discovered to avoid injury to its residents and other locals, declined to comment for this story. The IAA, which has jurisdiction over the antiquities found in the tomb itself, has also declined to comment.

The fates of Dr. Nevon and Mr. Geller are yet to be determined.

• • • •

THE BLOOMFIELD LIBRARY for the Humanities and Social Sciences, on the Mt. Scopus campus of Hebrew University where Uri taught, is north of the city of Jerusalem. I was in the Current

Periodicals Reading Room on the third floor of the library, in search of documentation for what Uri called "the incident": his and Lev's break-in of the Talpiot tomb. Local news outlets must have covered the story, but multiple searches of online archives that morning turned up nothing. Perhaps I'd find what I was looking for at the library.

The receptionist at the Help Desk told me that the Jerusalem Post, the city's English-language daily newspaper, would be my best bet for finding articles dealing with the break-in of the tomb. Given the non-threatening yet ominous phone calls Uri and I had recently received, I was hesitant to ask for help or make my presence known any more than I had to, but what other choice did I have in this case? The Internet had proven useless, and besides, I thought, what were the chances that this young college student knew or even cared what I was up to? She no doubt had problems of her own, and probably couldn't care less about this American stranger asking for her help.

She typed a query into her computer, disappeared for a few moments to search for my request, and re-emerged with two pieces of microfilm.

There were a handful of people in the room on this Friday afternoon. Some read quietly at wooden tables or oversized fabric chairs that were scattered throughout the room; others were picking through print journals and newspapers housed on long rows of shelves. From my vantage point, seated behind a microfilm machine tucked into a corner in the back of the room, I could see the entire third floor of the library.

I scanned the room when I finished reading the first story about "the incident." A few more people had trickled in, including a middle-aged man dressed in black seated at the table nearest to me, some twenty feet away. He was wearing black sunglasses and seemed to be engrossed in the magazine he was reading.

I switched out the first piece of microfilm for the second, hoping this article would tell me what had happened to Lev and Uri. I was surprised to discover from the first newspaper article that Lev had initially lied to police at the scene and said he was alone. And Uri, who could have easily hidden inside the tomb and allowed Lev to take the fall, emerged to confess his role in the break-in. Their bond must be much deeper than they cared to admit, for a professor and his student to display such acts of complete selflessness. More than anything else—more than how they managed to gain access to the cave, more than why they felt compelled to break the law to explore the tomb—the fact that they were both ready to sacrifice for each other, endeared them to me all the more. What were these two men to each other? What role did they play in each others' lives?

I scanned the other film. After a few minutes of searching, the fates of Uri and Lev became clear.

Jerusalem Post

December 10, 2007

FATES DECIDED FOR TALPIOT TOMB INVADERS

Judgment was handed down yesterday in the case of the Talpiot tomb invaders, two local men who executed a successful break-in at the cave on the outskirts of Jerusalem that a recent documentary claims is the lost resting place of Jesus Christ.

Dr. Uri Nevon, professor and biblical scholar at Hebrew University, was suspended from his teaching duties. It is unknown if he will ever return. Lev Geller, a shopkeeper's son from Old City, was temporarily expelled from Hebrew University, where he had been a freshman business major.

Despite public speculation that Dr. Nevon and Mr. Geller had help gaining access to the tomb, the police insist the men acted alone.

"These two men are smart," said Jerusalem police station chief Benjamin Schwarz. "They didn't need help doing what they did. This is an open-and-shut case."

• • • •

IT APPEARED THAT JUSTICE was swift yet merciful for Uri and Lev. Although job suspension and expulsion from school were tough pills to swallow, neither situation seemed permanent. Uri wasn't fired, and Lev's expulsion, it seemed, was temporary. It could've been a lot worse. Like, jail time worse. Like, permanent criminal record worse.

I contemplated this as I packed up my things to leave the library, and thought about visiting Uri. I was within easy walking distance of his office, but I decided against it. I didn't know his schedule, and even if he wasn't in the middle of a lecture, an unannounced visit would be inconsiderate. Plus, the day we were at Lev's shop, we agreed that being seen together would be risky. It was clear Uri and I were being tailed, and no doubt Lev was, too. Best to let Uri contact me.

I returned the two pieces of microfilm to the secretary at the Help Desk, thanked her for her help, and exited the library.

I took a sherut back into town, to a taxi stand in the Jewish Quarter mere paces from the Western Wall. From here I walked a few blocks on the narrow Tiferet Yisrael Street, back to the café where Uri and I met and discussed Mary Magdalene over falafels.

I ordered a falafel to go from the café. I couldn't resist the soft pita bread wrapped around deep-fried mashed chick peas smothered in Israeli salad and spicy sauce. I silently thanked Uri for introducing these to me, paid for my lunch and set off walking again.

That's when I saw him. The man in black from the library. He was leaning against a building about a half of a block away.

When I first saw him at the library, he was sitting at a table a short distance from me reading a magazine. Had he still been there when I left the library? I retraced my steps in my mind as I walked and concluded that no, the middle-aged man dressed all in black was gone when I left. The table where he'd been sitting was empty.

I wouldn't have thought anything of this average-looking man had he not been wearing dark sunglasses inside. And now, as I continued walking on Tiferet Yisrael Street, inching closer to him with every step, it was the sunglasses that gave him away.

Suddenly he ducked behind a building up ahead of me and disappeared. I stopped for a moment, contemplating where he'd gone and what I should do. Was he following me? I shook that thought from my head but thought it best to proceed with caution just in case. A crowded place to blend in and hide in plain sight was in order, so I turned left and made my way to Hurva square. Once there, I found a bench in the shade to eat my lunch.

I finished my falafel and decided to check out the sites of Hurva Square, just as a distant church bell was chiming two o'clock.

A maze of narrow, winding streets went off in all directions from the center of Hurva Square, which is the heart of the Jewish Quarter. Locals sat at outdoor cafes, relaxing with friends and family, and a few tourists strolled about. The area is dominated by several ornately decorated synagogues from the 17th century, and I walked around snapping pictures of their stone exteriors.

There was much to see in this small yet historically rich area of the Jewish Quarter, including the Cardo. In the Byzantine era, the Cardo was Jerusalem's main thoroughfare, and has since been converted to a covered shopping arcade. But I had no time to shop. I had work to do. It was time to go.

I started heading north on foot along Jewish Quarter Road, which ended at an area containing several souks. If I continued north through this marketplace district, I'd eventually cross Via Dolorosa Road, pass through the Muslim Quarter and out one of the gates that led into modern New City.

Despite being surrounded by the bustle of commerce and tourist groups, I felt uneasy after several minutes of walking. I turned around, still unable to shake the feeling of being followed.

That's when I saw him again. The man in black from the library. He was about fifty feet behind me, walking casually as if window shopping.

Perhaps the first two times I saw him were coincidence. But the third time? This had to be intentional. It seemed shady to me. And it meant danger.

I picked up my pace to a speed walk. But glancing back I noticed that the man in black was still right behind me, keeping pace, his intentions unclear. Would he eventually catch up to me when he thought the time was right? And if so, then what? Would he grab me and threaten me and then let me go? Or would he kidnap me, walk me through the streets of Jerusalem to some secret location and hold me hostage? Who was he, and what did he want?

I was jogging now, crossing David Street into a maze of stalls showcasing fruits, vegetables, baked goods, wine, clothing, meats, cheeses, house wares and souvenirs. Maybe I would lose the man in black in here, under these covered markets swarming with vendors and tourists. I weaved in and out of the various aisles, continuing north, not staying in any one aisle for too long, and not pausing at any of the stalls. Eventually, though, my feet ached and my chest heaved under the stress. I was perspiring and my head grew too dizzy to continue. I had to stop for a few minutes.

After seeing no sign of the man in black for awhile, I stopped to rest at one of the stalls. The vendor and his customer looked at me curiously as I pretended to admire his wares. How I must have looked to them, red-faced and out of breath, occasionally glancing around urgently and flinching at anyone who came near me.

After a few minutes, the coast was clear. I thought I had lost him.

Just then, however, I saw him over my left shoulder, half-hidden by trinkets and souvenirs that hung from the ceiling of a nearby stall. There was no mistaking his large black sunglasses. He was looking for me, his head swiveling side-to-side, scanning the crowd.

I started walking, slowly at first, until I was around the corner and hopefully out of view. Then I started jogging, until I emerged through the exit of the marketplace onto the street outside Alexander Hospice, a place of worship for the Russian Orthodox Church.

I stopped to catch my breath. Looking around to see if I'd given the man in black the slip, I noticed a large crowd of people coming down the street toward me. They were crying and chanting and praying, a frenzy of emotions. There were men of faith dressed in robes, women draped in long swathes of cloth, and tourists quietly and respectfully walking along taking it all in. And there was a man in front leading them all, struggling to hold a large wooden cross on his shoulders. The crowd came closer until eventually it enveloped me on all sides and I was lost in a sea of people. Some of them ignored me, and some were too enraptured to see me and brushed against me as they passed by on their way to who-knows-where.

Just then, as the crowd was moving on, I made the connection. These people were participating in the walk along the Via Dolorosa, or Stations of the Cross, the supposed last steps of Jesus Christ.

Every Friday afternoon Franciscan friars walk the winding, narrow streets along the route to all fourteen stations; religious pilgrims and devotees participate to help recreate the events of the story and to help them identify with Christ's suffering.

I hadn't the time to reflect on the activity in front of me, however, because the man in black was approaching. If I continued to stand still he would catch up and overtake me in a matter of seconds, and then who knew what would happen? I couldn't stay here, out in the open, exposed, vulnerable. Where could I go?

Just then I remembered something I'd read in my guidebook about the Alexander Hospice, the 19th century church I currently found myself standing in front of.

When the hospice was founded, it was already known to contain the ruins of a 4th century stone building, a building that just happens to be the most sacred site in all Christendom. It is the place where the Messiah supposedly died, was buried, and was then resurrected. This meant I was within steps of ground zero of the Christian faith, a place where people go to worship and pray and give thanks. It was a place that would be swarming with throngs of people on the outside, but would be respectfully quiet and tranquil on the inside. A place that I thought would be safe.

The crowd was in the last stages of its walk along the Via Dolorosa, and was on its way to this building. And that's where I had to go, too. If I could only use them as cover...

Instinctively I started to run, as fast as I could, quickly catching up with the crowd of people on their way to the same place I wanted to go. Looking over my shoulder one last time I saw that the man in black was no longer following me. He stood outside the Alexander Hospice, the place where I'd just stood, his hands balled into fists. Perhaps he realized where I was going, and knew that he could not follow. Where I was going, there would be no disturbing the peace.

I approached the courtyard and pushed my way through the crowds, crossing the threshold into the dimly lit interior. A sense of relief came over me, then awe as I took in my surroundings—the ornate alters, the colored glass, the finely chiseled stones.

Then the irony set in. I, a person devoid of all religious faith, had found sanctuary in a building devoted to Jesus Christ: the Church of the Holy Sepulchre.

CHAPTER FOURTEEN

There were emails waiting for me from Lisa and Jenny. Jenny's email was mostly business, seeing if I was making progress on this new novel idea, and filling me in on sales on the others. Lisa's email, meanwhile, was all personal. Was I safe? Was I learning a lot and seeing a lot of cool things? Had I met any eligible men?

I took a few minutes to respond to them, keeping it brief, because I had an interview scheduled this afternoon with a professor that I needed to prepare for. I'd respond in detail later, once I had the mental capacity to focus on something other than ancient tombs and my little crush on Dr. Uri Nevon.

Half an hour later, I found myself back in familiar territory, on the Mt. Scopus campus of Hebrew University. I was here to interview Associate Professor Ariel Feldman.

I had found her listed on the Hebrew University website faculty directory, one of several websites I checked out during my initial research back in the States. Hebrew University was one of the top universities in all of Israel, so I was sure the school was a repository for skilled archaeologists, biblical scholars, and learned professors.

Ms. Feldman was one of several professors I e-mailed before arriving in Jerusalem. It took her awhile to respond (I'd already met Lev and Uri and was well on my way to seeing the Talpiot tomb) but I decided that since she'd taken the time to respond and seemed genuinely interested, I should at least meet with her and see what she had to say. It never hurts to get as many professional opinions as possible.

There was no picture of the professor next to her bio, but his office address was listed, so I knew precisely where to go to meet her for our scheduled meeting. A few e-mail exchanges had established this day and time as the most agreeable for her schedule.

Had I seen Uri's name on the Hebrew University website, I would've e-mailed him as well. But he was not listed in the faculty directory. Perhaps his name had been removed when he was suspended from teaching. Once I found out who he was, thanks to Lev's referral, I Googled Uri's name. At the top of the search results was Cambridge University and a link to a press release from 2006 announcing his visit to campus for a guest lecture. It was this press release, with Uri's bio at the bottom, that I had printed and kept among all my notes.

I climbed the steps to the second floor and wound my way down several hallways to Ms. Feldman's office, reviewing her short bio as I went: "Ariel Feldman is an Associate Professor at Hebrew University who specializes in New Testament archeology."

Her office door was halfway open, and I could see a woman inside. She was standing behind a metal desk, sorting some papers that sat on top. I knocked lightly and peeked my head in.

The woman looked up at me. She had long reddish-brown hair and hazel eyes. She wore a tan skirt and matching jacket.

"May I help you?" she asked.

"My name is Mara Beltane. I'm looking for Professor Feldman."

"I'm Professor Feldman," she said, waving me inside. We shook hands and she motioned for me to have a seat in the chair in front of her desk.

Her office was small and cluttered, with two shelves against the right-hand wall overflowing with books. A window behind the desk overlooked a green swath of grass.

She folded her hands on the desk and looked at me with a face that betrayed her age. Small wrinkles creased the corners of her eyes and a few short gray hairs peeked out from her temple, swimming in a river of reddish brown hair that cascaded over her shoulders and down her back.

She had skin the color of lightly-tanned leather and a figure as shapely as an African gazelle. And her makeup was perfect. She was undoubtedly the most beautiful woman I'd seen in Jerusalem.

But that glare! It was intimidating and demanding, like she could convince anyone to do her bidding using the power of her eyes alone.

"You mentioned in your email you're a writer?" she asked.

"A novelist."

"Anything I would've read?"

"I write what's considered women's fiction. Lighthearted stories about young women trying to navigate life and love. That kind of thing."

"I see," Ariel said, nodding. "But you mentioned you're writing a novel about the Talpiot tomb. That's quite a departure from what you usually write..."

I sat for a moment, trying to decide if she was accusing me of something or just legitimately curious.

"I've always been interested in religious history," I said. "And I've been needing to expand my writing horizons, so I decided to put my minor in biblical studies to good use."

All this was true. I had a Bachelor's in English, with which I thought I could do a myriad of things—teach and write being my top two choices. Both of which panned out. And when my college advisor told me I should probably declare a minor, I chose biblical studies. I didn't think too long or hard about it because frankly, I didn't think minors served any practical purpose in your future professional career. So I chose biblical studies, simply because, due to my family history, I'd had an interest in Christian history from a young age. I thought it would be something cool to learn. End of story.

Turns out, given my current situation, and where I found myself, I might be able to use that minor, after all.

"So what are you researching, exactly?" Ariel asked. "What's the plot?"

"I don't have the entire plot outlined yet," I said. "But it centers around the Talpiot tomb being the final resting place of Jesus of Nazareth."

"That book could end up being quite the thrilling page-turner..." She blinked but never took her eyes from me. Not once did she look way, lower her eyes, appear distracted, or back down from a comment.

"What do you think, Professor Feldman?" I asked. "Do you think it could be true?"

Ariel squinted at me, and I wasn't sure if it was because she was contemplating my question, sizing me up, or both. Her expression softened.

"No, I don't think the tomb is the final resting place of Jesus," she said. "For all the reasons you've probably read about during your research."

"Fair enough," I said.

There was a pause and finally, she said, "A dear friend and colleague of mine—also a professor here—used to ask me why I found it so hard to believe in the Talpiot tomb."

"What was your answer?" I asked.

"I asked him how he found it so easy to believe."

"He believed it was real?"

"I think he wanted it to be real, but deep down I think he had his doubts."

I pulled my notebook from my bag and rummaged around for a pen, in case we ever got to the point in this conversation where'd I'd need to take notes. When I returned my attention to Ariel, she was staring at me again with those commanding eyes.

"Perhaps you've heard of my colleague," she said. "Professor Uri Nevon?"

I flinched at the sound of his name, then panicked thinking that she could detect the look of surprise on my face. Tread cautiously, I reminded myself. I don't know her. I don't know what she knows. I don't know *who* she knows.

"Nevon," I said. "Sounds familiar."

"I thought you might have come across his name during your research."

"I might have...?" I pretended to be confused, as if I'd done so much research already, encountered enough people, to cause everything to blur together.

"He has an interest in the Talpiot tomb. He's the one who asked me how I found it so hard to believe."

"Oh, I see..."

"You should look him up and contact him."

"I will, thanks," I said, my heart thumping. "Do you know him well?"

I scribbled Uri's name down in my notebook, along with some random notes to make it appear as if I was learning new information. Ariel continued to speak as I wrote.

"Yes, we know each other well. Plus we work in the same department here." She sighed, as if reminiscing old memories. "And in spite of it all, and specifically what personally happened between us, we remained friends. I'm grateful for that."

My head snapped up. In spite of what happened? My heart was thumping harder now, and it was getting tougher to pretend.

We stared at each other a moment. I felt like Ariel was waiting for me to say something, to respond to her dangling carrot. But I was struggling for words. Why would she mention Uri in such a way? Why was she trying to bait me with personal information? Tread cautiously, Mara...

"I'm...I'm not sure how to respond to that..." I started.

Ariel sighed, looking at me with what approximated pity. "Uri didn't tell you," she said.

"Professor Nevon and I have never met. But I appreciate you mentioning him, and I will look him up." I said this firmly, as if it mattered at this point. Somehow this woman, whom I'd just met, knew that I'd met Uri. And Lord only knew what else she knew...

Ariel smiled. "May I call you Mara?"

I resisted the urge to make up an excuse as to why I had to leave. I nodded instead and said nothing.

"Uri and I—" she started.

Just then there was a loud knock on the door. I jumped in my seat, startled, and whipped my head around to see a young woman standing in the doorway, holding several three-ring binders.

"Ziva, don't forget the meeting," the young woman said. "It starts in ten minutes."

"Yes, thank you," the professor said, looking at her watch. "I'll be right there."

Ziva? That was the name of the mysterious woman Lev and Uri had been talking about in the shop the other day. They asked one another when they had spoken to her last. And both confessed they spoke to her only once in awhile. She definitely had relationships of some sort with both of them. Was the woman who sat in front of me the same Ziva?

"My personal assistant," the professor whispered as the young lady closed the door. Then she looked at me curiously. "Are you alright, Mara? You look like you've seen a ghost."

"I thought your name was Ariel?" I asked, ignoring her statement.

"Ziva is my middle name," she explained. "Only a handful of people call me that. Friends, family, close colleagues..."

If the woman sitting across from me was the same Ziva who Lev and Uri were talking about, then they must know her well enough to call her by her middle name. So how did they all know each other?

"I must go to this meeting," the professor said. She wrote a phone number down on a small scrap of paper and handed it to me. "Here's Uri's phone number. Although, I think—" She stopped herself. Then she stood and straightened her skirt. "Uri will tell you everything you need to know. As well as everything you *want* to know. Now, please excuse me." She stepped out from behind the desk and made her way to the door.

But I couldn't let her go. She hinted at a past with Uri, intentionally, and I couldn't let her off so easily, without an answer. Why would she have dangled that carrot earlier if she had no intention of telling me anything? Simply to be cruel?

I gathered my things and stood up quickly. "Wait! You started to say something...about Uri...before we were interrupted...."

Ariel, Ziva, whoever...stared at me a moment, as if contemplating whether or not to tell me about Uri. If there was, in fact, anything to divulge. Perhaps the look on her face meant she was searching for a way to tell me the truth, or perhaps it meant she was digging for a lie.

"I really have to get to this meeting..." she said.

"You're the one who threw his name out there," I reminded her, a bit too harshly. I screwed up my face in a silent apology. I softened my voice. "Two minutes, please..."

Arield sighed. "Uri and I were engaged. The Talpiot tomb drove a wedge between us when he became obsessed with the idea of breaking into it. I broke off the engagement, and several weeks later he was arrested for breaking into the tomb."

I'd asked for two minutes, but it only took her fifteen seconds to sum up what happened. And those fifteen seconds prompted more questions then she would probably have time to answer. But I pushed to get my two minutes.

"I've already met Uri," I confessed.

"I know."

"How do you know?"

"It doesn't matter."

Well, it kind of did matter, but I let it go.

"Does the name Lev Geller mean anything to you?" I asked.

"Lev is my brother."

I was quiet for a moment, as it all sank in, as the puzzle pieces fell into place. Ariel looked at her watch.

"Why did it seem like you wanted to tell me about your relationship with Uri?" I asked.

"Because you will fall for him, if you haven't already. It's easy to do. So I wanted you to be prepared in case that happens."

"We've only just met. I'm not in Jerusalem for long..."

Ariel smiled knowingly, without explanation, then changed the subject. "If you are planning to do what I think you are, be careful."

Did she also know about our plans to access the Talpiot tomb? How?

"Is that a warning or a threat or...?" I asked.

"I must go," Ariel said. She shook my hand and opened the door for me to leave. "Thank you for coming."

I thanked Ariel for her time, knowing I'd get nothing more from her. And as I left her office, I noticed a man standing about fifty feet down the hallway in the opposite direction from which I needed to go. His face was partially obscured by the newspaper he was pretending to read, but I saw enough to know who it was.

The man in black.

CHAPTER FIFTEEN

The pieces were starting to fit together. Uri had been engaged to Ziva. Ziva was Lev's sister. Lev had been a student of Uri's and almost became his brother-in-law. It explained Lev and Uri's relationship, their mutual respect for one another.

So who was the man in black? He had been watching me at the library and followed me through the streets of Jerusalem. And just now he had been standing outside Ziva's office. Why was he following me? Did Ziva know who he was? Did she know he'd been standing outside her office? He was obviously a piece of this big puzzle, but I hadn't figured out yet where he fit.

I desperately wanted to see the complete picture. I needed answers. And at the moment, Uri was the only one who could help me. I just hoped the man in black wouldn't follow me.

I left Ziva's office and sped-walked across campus to Uri's building, glancing at my watch.

2:30 p.m.

I thought I heard him mention the other day that he had classes until early afternoon most days. I was hoping early afternoon meant 2:30.

When I approached the lecture hall I slowed to a walk. Kids were filtering out of the room. I was in luck. Class had just been dismissed. I hovered near the entrance until the last student exited and then stood in the doorway, peeking in. Uri was alone, standing at the lectern, packing up his briefcase. I knocked on the door and he turned toward me, startled.

"Oh, hi Mara," he said. "I wasn't expecting you."

"I hope you don't mind. I know it's risky but I was in the neighborhood."

"That's okay. I think we're safe here. Come on in."

I looked up and down the hallway, making sure I didn't see anything suspicious before entering.

Uri looked at me curiously as I approached the lectern.

"Is everything all right?" he asked.

I took a deep breath and proceeded. "I just met Ziva."

"Oh." His eyes darted around the room for a minute, then he looked me deeply in the eyes. "Perhaps we should talk."

• • • •

I ALWAYS THOUGHT THE phrase "We need to talk" and its close cousins, "We should talk," "Can we talk?" and "Let's talk" should be reserved for the moments when two peoples' line of communication had broken down so severely that the only way it could begin to be repaired was by uttering a variation of those words. The phrase would serve as a primer, a way to prepare you for what was about to occur: A serious, no-bullshit conversation in which both sides aired their grievances and attempted to make amends so they could move on with their lives. That way, there were no surprises. When you heard those words, you knew what to expect—an uncomfortable yet necessary conversation. That seems fair and just to me.

It's kind of like a pre-show at a Disney attraction. You sit through a silly song or listen to an animated character tell a story that serves as an introduction to what you are about to experience. The pre-show sets up the premise of the ride so you know what to expect.

The pre-show, in other words, is your "we need to talk" moment.

Thomas and I had been married a year when he first said, "We need to talk." At the time I had just acquired my agent Jenny and was attempting to sell my first novel. It was an exciting time for me, and a busy time, as I was teaching by day and writing novels at night. Thomas was happy for me and very supportive. Everything was as it should be. We were happy.

We were putting groceries away on that Saturday morning when Thomas said those fateful words.

"That sounds serious," I said, handing him a bag of frozen peas.

He didn't smile or say anything. He just continued to pile items into the freezer.

I felt my stomach drop and my hands started to shake. "What do you want to talk about?"

"We need to start planning our future," he said. A box of waffles and some hamburgers disappeared into the freezer.

"I thought we had a plan."

"We did. But you're getting more serious about your writing career, and that could change the plan."

The plan for our lives involved steady careers, children, social lives, and travel. I was starting to sense that he suddenly didn't think there was room for anything else—like a writing career on the side.

"I don't think our lives will change much," I said. "The plan is still solid."

"We're both already pretty busy with our primary careers," Thomas said, closing the freezer door. All the groceries were put away. He drifted over to the kitchen table and sat down. "Once we start having kids..." he said it more to himself than to me.

I sank into my usual chair opposite him.

"You are happy for me, right?" I asked.

"Of course, Mara. I'm proud of you. And happy that you're pursuing your passion..."

But...

There was a but there, a big one, and I didn't sense it. I was too wrapped up in my own wants to even have noticed his. While I was wanting a life outside our marriage, something to call my own—he was doubling down on life inside our marriage.

And that, I believe, is the precise moment our marriage started to fail. One year in, and already a crack. I hadn't seen the deeper meaning of our conversation and the serious implications it would have over the next couple of years.

Our talk had taken the form of a conversation about my then side career as a novelist, but that's not what was really happening. Thomas was thinking about something else altogether. He was subconsciously planting the seeds of parenthood.

The first time Thomas and I needed to have a serious talk and failed to get to the heart of the matter, a crack formed. The *last* time Thomas and I needed to have a serious talk and were unsuccessful, a handful of years later, the crack split wide open into a deep, irreparable chasm, one Thomas felt helpless to fix. And that is when he left me.

So when Uri, my new Israeli companion whom I'd known only a few days, said we needed to talk, I had no idea what to expect. We were in a lecture hall, class had just been dismissed, and we sat side by side in the front row of seats.

"You met Ziva," Uri said.

"I met Ariel Feldman," I clarified. "A professor I had emailed prior to arriving in Jerusalem to see if she would be willing to be interviewed about the Talpiot tomb for a book I was writing."

"I see..." Uri said.

"She is the Ziva you and Lev had been talking about?"

"Yes."

"I had no idea she was Ziva until literally a half-hour ago when we met."

"How did it go?"

"Not great," I said. "She knows about our plan."

Uri stiffened and his eyes widened. "What?"

"I mean, I didn't tell her. She just...knows somehow. You suspected that. You said so yourself that day in Lev's store."

"What did she say?"

"She told me that Lev is her brother. And that you two were...engaged."

Uri said nothing at first. For the first time since I met him, he was at a loss for words.

"She didn't go into detail about your relationship or how it ended," I offered.

Uri smiled and I smiled and then there were no more words between us for what seemed like minutes, but it was really only about ten seconds. I glanced over at the white board and scanned the notes Uri had written on it, a half-English, half-Hebrew jumble of words and phrases in black marker.

"What did she say that made you suspect that she knows about our plan?" Uri finally said, pulling my attention away from the white board and back to the subject at hand.

"It was more of a warning. Something along the lines of, 'be careful doing what I think you're going to do.'"

Naturally I left out the part where Ziva prophesized I would fall for Uri. That was girl-talk Uri didn't need to hear. And although I thought Ziva was right, I wasn't ready to process that just yet. Those were emotions best left for another time.

"Perhaps I should've told you who she was that day in the store," Uri said.

"Why didn't you? I mean, your relationship is none of my business, but you suspected she knew about our plan."

"We were discussing who else you'd talked to, and who *those* people would've told. When it comes to the Talpiot tomb, news travels fast."

"I told Abigail."

Uri was shaking his head the minute her name came out of her mouth. "I trust her. She wouldn't say a word to anyone. Ziva found out another way, and it doesn't even matter how at this point."

"She did ask me a ton of questions," I said, laughing. "It was like she was interviewing me rather than the other way around."

Uri smiled wanly. "Yes, she does that."

"Very intimidating," I added.

Uri smiled and said nothing.

"But she didn't threaten me or anything," I continued. "It was like she discreetly acknowledged the elephant in the room and moved on."

"I never thought the two of you would meet," Uri said, quietly.

"What?"

"That's the other reason I didn't mention Ziva," Uri said, louder. "I didn't think you'd meet each other." Was that a nervous smile?

"Why would that matter?"

"Because...I know she can be intimidating, like you said. And I wouldn't want her to make you feel uncomfortable."

"I can handle her," I joked. "And besides, we'll be trying to avoid her now that we suspect she knows our plan."

"Very true."

"Unless you and her stay in touch...?" I took a risk with that question, asking something that was really none of my business, and telling myself it was for the good of our plan, not to quell the subtle jealousy I felt bubbling inside me.

Uri waved off the question. "That is not an issue. We hardly speak."

Relief oozed out of me in that moment. I allowed myself the briefest of seconds to feel it and then moved on.

"Well, it's not Ziva I'm worried about, anyway" I said. "It's the man in black."

"Who?"

"I don't know who he is. I just saw him standing outside Ziva's office. Suspicious-looking character."

"Describe him to me."

"Mid-forties, I'd say. Tall and broad-shouldered. Buzz cut black hair with some gray." I paused a moment. "Oh, and every time I saw him he was wearing black clothes and big black sunglasses."

"You've seen him more than once?"

"I saw him the first time a couple of days ago when I was doing research at the Bloomfield Library. He must've been following me because I saw him later that afternoon at Hurva Square. And then... he chased me."

Uri said up straight in his chair, his eyes large and unblinking. "What?"

"He chased me through Hurva Square," I said. "I thought I'd lost him inside a souk, but he tracked me down. I finally gave him the slip at the Church of the Holy Sepulchre."

Uri reached across the armrest that separated us and gently took my hand. "Mara, why didn't you tell me?"

I looked down at Uri's hand as it held mine, silently wishing he'd never let go, and wondered why I hadn't told Uri that I was chased through the streets of Jerusalem.

I hadn't kept the story from him on purpose. I hadn't intended to *not* tell him. It just got pushed into my subconscious somehow, along with all my memories of Thomas, and my attraction to Uri, and my sudden disdain for a beautiful Israeli woman I hardly knew.

"I'm so sorry you had to go through that," Uri said. "Are you all right?"

"I'm...I'm fine," I said, distracted by the warmth of Uri's touch. I was still staring at our hands, wrapped together in my lap, when he pulled his hand loose and placed it in his own lap.

"So who is this man in black?" I asked, my head still lowered to hide my flushed face.

"Benjamin Schwarz, the head of the Jerusalem district of the Israel Police."

I recognized the name. Benjamin Schwarz was the man quoted in the Talpiot tomb articles from the Jerusalem Post that I'd read at the Bloomfield Library. He was quoted in the articles as saying that he believed Uri and Lev had no help breaking into the tomb. They had acted alone, he'd said rather emphatically. Open and shut case.

"And he's Ziva's husband," Uri added.

My head shot up. "Husband?"

"Benjamin arrested me and Lev the night we broke into the Talpiot tomb," Uri said. "And I believe he's responsible for the crank calls you and I received."

"Whoa. How can you be sure of that? The person didn't say anything to either of us."

"Ziva," was all Uri said. He seemed so sure.

"Are you saying that Ziva told you her husband was spying on us?"

"Yes."

"Why would she do that?"

"She was trying to warn me about what might happen. That we'd be arrested again."

"How did she warn you, exactly? By just coming out and telling you that we'd be arrested?"

"Well, yes," Uri said, as if the answer to my question seemed so simple and obvious. "But there's more to the story..."

"She obviously told you after we met at Lev's store, because that's when you first suspected she was somehow involved, and before I met her today..." I was working out the timeline verbally and not expecting an answer from Uri. But he gave one anyway.

"She called me yesterday. I was going to tell you everything, but I didn't know when I'd see you next. I couldn't risk calling or texting. And then you met her today and found out before I had the chance to tell you myself." There was sadness in his voice, laced with guilt.

"So your government suspects we're going to access the Talpiot tomb and the police are tailing us because of it..." I sighed deeply. "That sure did escalate quickly."

"It's unfortunate, and I'm sorry, Mara."

"It's OK. It's not your fault. I'm the one who came here and started digging my nose in where it doesn't belong."

"I did warn you," he said, sternly but with a smile. "I said this wouldn't be easy. And, most importantly, I said that once we started there was no turning back."

"I remember. I haven't changed my mind."

And I hadn't. I knew there was no going back. We could pull the plug, but there'd still be suspicion following us like a shadow. We might still be followed, watched, or questioned, whether we forged ahead or not. I might be detained when I left the country. We could go silent and go underground in order to forward our mission, or pull the plug and admit what our plan had been. No matter what we decided to do, the outcome would probably still be the same: The three of us would forever be under the watchful eye of someone, somewhere.

Lev and Uri were already living that reality, so the risk for them was especially high.

But both of them were determined to help me so, despite my misgivings, I had to move forward. For them and for me. To finish my mission in Jerusalem, and to make their sacrifice worth it. And I was so close...

"Now, finally, you understand the urgency of our mission," Uri said.

I nodded, still allowing everything to sink in.

"What are you doing the day after tomorrow?" he asked.

"Well, I have a spa treatment in the morning, and then I'm meeting some girlfriends for lunch..." I said, and Uri laughed. "I'm not doing anything the day after tomorrow."

"It's settled then," he said, a look of optimism and determination on his face. "We see the Talpiot tomb in two days."

"What about tomorrow?" I said. "I thought there was urgency."

"Lev and I need one more day to make final arrangements. Besides, there is something you must see first. Something of great importance."

"What it is?" I asked, ignoring his statement about final arrangements because, really, I didn't need to know. The details would surface when they were meant to. I would find out when I was supposed to.

Uri tilted his head and smiled. "Meet me tomorrow and I will show you."

CHAPTER SIXTEEN

The local radio station came back from commercial break to deliver a news brief. The male DJ's voice was deep and serious:

Several protesters, policemen and worshippers were injured late yesterday afternoon when violence erupted during a Palestinian protest over the continuing Israeli settlement building along the West Bank.

Police stormed the Temple Mount, a holy site for both Jews and Muslims, when Muslim protestors started hurling rocks and bottles, and taunted Jewish worshippers. The worshippers were evacuated from the Western Wall plaza at the foot of the hilltop compound, but not before several of them were cut by shards of flying glass. Police released tear gas and fired rubber bullets to disperse the violent protesters. It took several hours for the smoke to clear and before police had the situation under control. All told, two policemen sustained minor injuries and—

• • • •

URI SWITCHED OFF THE car radio. I remained quiet, unsure if I should comment on the chaos that frequently erupts between the warring Jewish and Palestinian populations.

"Are you excited?" Uri said, eyeing me from the driver's side of his car.

We were on our way to a storage facility in Beth Shemesh, within the industrial zone of Jerusalem, and I doubted that we'd be able to gain access without special permission.

"I'm excited," I said, "and a little concerned. Are we just going to waltz in there?"

"They know we're coming," Uri said. "I made arrangements. This place is not easy to find or recognize, but it's not off limits."

"That's not what I heard."

"You've probably heard the warehouse is top secret and purposefully hidden."

"That's exactly what I heard."

"A common misconception. Everyone loves a good conspiracy theory." We both laughed. "In reality," Uri continued, "anyone can request a visit to the IAA warehouse for research. And I've been here enough times that the staff knows me pretty well."

The staff in question, all employees of the Israeli Antiquities Authority, guarded over some of the most precious cultural antiquities discovered in the Holy Land, including the six inscribed ossuaries pulled from the Talpiot tomb.

It was these ossuaries that we were on our way to see.

When the Talpiot tomb was excavated in 1980, the bones that were found inside were reburied according to Jewish tradition. The six inscribed ossuaries were archived and put in storage at the IAA warehouse in Beth Shemesh, where they've remained to this day. The IAA believed the Talpiot tomb ossuaries to be common, typical for the time period they were from. Hundreds just like them were stacked floor to ceiling within the walls of the warehouse—and this warehouse was the second most important stop on my itinerary.

We pulled into a parking lot in front of a large concrete building with a white garage door. Above the door was a white sign with blue lettering in Hebrew and English, declaring that this building was an IAA facility.

We entered the building and Uri and a male guard greeted each other with a handshake and what sounded like pleasantries in Hebrew. The guard stepped aside and allowed us to pass, and we were on our way.

Uri led me through room after room of artifacts: Small corners filled with delicate pottery shards and fine jewelry; climate-controlled rooms for metallic objects; an entire room just for glass; and large storerooms with metal shelves stacked floor to ceiling with large vessels and pieces of architecture.

There were many people at work—examining ceramic shards under a microscope, wheeling large stone slabs through the hallways, dusting off pieces of pottery with fine-bristled brushes. All around me progress was being made, history was being uncovered...life, discovered and dissected as I watched.

We paused in a hallway.

"This building is officially called the National Treasures Storerooms," Uri said.

"There are enough treasures here to fill a dozen museums."

"One million treasures, in fact. Each one archived electronically and arranged chronologically by place of origin. It is the largest facility of its kind in the Ancient East."

"These items should be in museums."

Uri shrugged as if he didn't have an answer, but he agreed with me nonetheless. "It's complicated," he said.

"Everything in Jerusalem is complicated," I chuckled. "So where's the ossuary storeroom?"

Uri waved a hand and asked me to follow him. "I left it for last."

We kept walking and eventually reached a large storeroom with fluorescent lights and seemingly endless rows of metal shelves stacked floor to ceiling with ossuaries. All the ossuaries dated from around the first century A.D., the time of Jesus of Nazareth, when the creation of stone bone boxes was being practiced. But what seemed like thousands of ossuaries to me, in fact, numbered only in the hundreds.

Uri watched me closely as I surveyed the room and its precious contents. Then he led the way forward.

He led me part way down an aisle and stopped, his eyes trained on an ossuary housed on a shelf about chest height. He placed his hand on it.

"This is the Marya ossuary," he said, shifting the bone box so that the front panel with the inscription on it was facing out. The inscription was centered on the upper half of the ossuary, near the rim. Uri said the letters as he traced his fingers over each one. "M-A-R-Y-A. You would know the name by its Latin origins: Maria, or Mary."

"As in Mary the mother of Jesus?" I asked playfully.

Uri smiled but didn't directly address my comment. "This ossuary is inscribed in Hebrew," he said. "Marya translated into Hebrew is Miriam. Most scholars and experts believe this is the ossuary of a Palestinian Jewish woman named Miriam. It was a very common name in Jesus' time."

"So, the fact that the ossuary of a woman named Miriam, or Mary, was found in the same tomb as an ossuary inscribed with the name Jesus son of Joseph is coincidence?"

Uri smiled but said nothing, and was on the move again. I barely had time to look at the Marya ossuary, let alone contemplate its significance before I was being ushered to a second ossuary.

"Yose," Uri said, pointing to the Hebrew inscription on one of the front panels. The inscription was positioned near the top, left of center. "Notice the similarity of this inscription with the Marya inscription."

I moved closer to the ossuary, until my nose just about touched the cold stone. Indeed, the inscriptions looked similar. They shared no letters, but each letter appeared to be the same width and depth, and spaced the same distance apart. It was as if both inscriptions were etched by the same hand, using the same instrument.

"Yose is a shortened form of Joseph," Uri said. "Kind of like a nickname. Today, everyone would call him Joe."

I thought about this a moment. "Jesus had a brother named Joseph."

"Yes, he did."

"Aren't there claims that the Yose ossuary is the bone box of Joseph, brother of Jesus?"

"Yes," Uri said. "And since we know that ossuaries were inscribed by family members of the deceased, if this is the bone box of Jesus' brother Joseph, it makes sense that it's etched with the name he most commonly went by in his family circle: Yose."

I pulled my notebook and a pen out of my bag and started taking notes.

The Yose ossuary was a good place to start in making an argument that the Talpiot tomb was real, and that the final resting place of Jesus of Nazareth had been found at long last.

"But putting Yose's nickname on his ossuary had a practical purpose too," Uri continued.

"And what was that?" I asked, still writing.

"It's possible that Yose's family inscribed this nickname on his bone box to distinguish him from Joseph, the name that appears on the *Jesus son of Joseph* ossuary."

"I see."

"Most scholars and historians treat Yose and Joseph as two separate people. But what if there's another possibility?"

I looked up at Uri, my pen in mid stroke. His eyebrows were raised and his hands were clenched together in front of him, as if he was about to burst from the excitement of this new revelation.

"Another possibility..." I repeated.

"If we are to believe the Talpiot tomb is the resting place of Jesus and his family, then we would expect to find Jesus' parents' ossuaries in the tomb. You could argue that the Marya ossuary, which you just saw, belonged to Jesus' mother, right?"

"Right."

"So then, where is Jesus' father, Joseph?"

"You wouldn't expect to find Joseph's ossuary in the Talpiot tomb because he wasn't from Jerusalem; he was from Nazareth," I said. "Isn't that Jewish law? That you are to be buried near your geographic origins?"

"Yes."

"Isn't that one of the main arguments detractors use to disprove the legitimacy of the Talpiot tomb? That Jesus' family wasn't even from Jerusalem?"

"Yes, but what if Joseph wasn't buried in Nazareth? What if his ossuary has been under our nose the whole time and we never knew it?"

"I don't understand."

"We've already determined that the name Yose is short for Joseph, and that Marya can be translated as Mary," Uri said. "And now we know that the Yose and Marya inscriptions were similar..."

Then it hit me. I suddenly knew what Uri was suggesting. "Do you think it's possible that the Yose ossuary belongs to Joseph, the father of Jesus?"

"Yes!" he exclaimed. "Think about it: The Yose ossuary and the Marya ossuary had similar inscriptions that look like they were written by the same hand in Hebrew, and they were found in the same tomb."

"The ossuaries *do* translate into Joseph and Mary..." I said, tapping my pen against my cheek as I contemplated the possibility of Jesus' parents' ossuaries having been found. "But still, those were two of the most popular names at the time of Jesus. It's like walking into a graveyard and finding side-by-side tombstones etched with the names William and Elizabeth. Who could tell how they were related, or if they were related at all?"

I was starting to sound like Tovah, the skeptical tour guide at the Rockefeller Museum.

"There's no way of knowing, Uri," I concluded.

"It's likely that Yose wasn't Jesus' father, but with no evidence to discredit it, no proof, it must remain a possibility, right? After all," he added, "the fate of your novel depends on it."

With that, Uri clutched my hand and led me to the next ossuary, around the corner from Yose's. He didn't have to rotate this ossuary because the inscription was on the narrow side facing out at us. Large

Hebrew letters were etched near the top of the rim, slightly off-center. Uri looked at me in that curious way of his, eyebrows raised, as if willing me to speak.

I stared at the inscription, knowing that I'd seen it before. I'd seen them all before. On television. In books. On the Internet. And now live, in the flesh, so to speak.

"Matia!" I said, reinvigorated about our mission, for which I had Uri to thank. I had so much to thank him for, and I didn't for the life of me know how I would ever repay him.

"Yes," Uri confirmed. "A shortened form of Matthias, or Matthew. This is the most misunderstood ossuary from the Talpiot tomb."

"Why?" I asked, flipping over a new page in my notebook.

"Family tombs were reserved for family members only, and there is no known Matthew in the Jesus family."

"What about the apostle Matthew?" I ventured a guess.

"There's no known biblical document that states they were related."

"No known document that has been *found*," I clarified. "With no evidence to discredit it..."

"...It must remain a possibility," Uri finished his own statement, smiling.

"What about the apostle Matthias, the one who was chosen to replace Judas Iscariot?" I asked, suddenly remembering another Matthew from the New Testament. "Is it possible he was related to Jesus? Could it be his ossuary that was found in the Talpiot tomb?"

Uri thought about this a minute. "Well, if they were related, that could explain Matthias' sudden promotion to Apostle after Judas' death."

"A classic example of nepotism, first-century style," I said, and we both laughed nervously.

Uri composed himself, and a look of seriousness came over his face.

"Mara, are you ready to move on?"

"We're leaving?" I asked.

"On the contrary," he said, taking a step toward me and gently taking my hand. "We're not going anywhere. We've only just begun."

• • • •

CHAPTER SEVENTEEN

"We've spoken in length already about this ossuary," Uri said, motioning to the most controversial ossuary found in the Talpiot tomb.

The authenticity of this bone box could make or break the case that the tomb was the final resting place of Jesus of Nazareth.

"Mariamene e Mara," I said, giving in to the urge to want to touch the ossuary. I placed a hand on the side of the ossuary facing me and stroked the cold stone. "Mary Magdalene."

"Well, maybe..." Uri said. "If we accept that two separate languages were inscribed on the bone box: Mariamene, written in Greek, and Mara, which is Hebrew."

"Mary the Master," I translated into English.

"Yes," Uri said. "But two languages on the same ossuary is very rare. Another rarity is an ossuary identifying a person with a title, such as master. And no evidence exists that shows Mary Magdalene was ever called 'Mary the Master.' So we must throw out those two options. Do you remember a third possibility I mentioned?"

"Yes," I said, removing my hand from the stone box. "Two women in the same ossuary: a Mariamene and a Mara. They could have been interred at different times, their names inscribed in different Greek scripts—one formal, one informal—by two different people. If this is true, then most likely the women were related."

"That's right. We know that Jesus had at least two sisters, one of which we think was named Mary."

"Which could mean that Mariamene and Mara were sisters-in-law: Mariamene, otherwise known as Mary Magdalene, being Jesus' wife, and Mara, also known as Mary, being Jesus' sister."

"If you accept the sisters-in-law option as the truth, it would allow the names to fall in place, leaving you with the possibility that the

Talpiot tomb is indeed the final resting place of Jesus and his family," Uri concluded. "This would be interesting fodder for your novel."

"Yes...my novel," I said, placing a hand on the ossuary once more and tracing my fingers over the inscription.

I had temporarily forgotten about researching my novel, my original reason for being here, in this storeroom, in Jerusalem. How could I forget the sacrifice I made to be here? The trouble that I—and Uri and Lev, as well—could still get in? The lengths to which Uri had gone to help me?

How important it all seemed in the beginning of my journey to prove to myself that I was more than just a chick-lit writer. How insatiable my need to reinvent myself and my career. How absolutely essential it was to me that I write a controversial, bestselling novel. A novel to end all novels. The one that would definitively prove that everything we thought we knew about Jesus' death was wrong.

Now, suddenly, it was gone—the need to prove that I could be someone else, the importance of reinventing my career, the essentialness of this controversial idea that could no sooner by proven than sold to the masses as the truth.

One thing was still present, however. Desire. Oh, there was desire, but not for a novel. The desire I felt was for a man. And as I looked up at him, saw his dark brown eyes, I felt it. I had lost my original reason for coming to Jerusalem, but I had found a reason to stay.

"...but it could also mean that the Mariamene and Mara in this ossuary were mother and daughter..." Uri was saying.

I regained my focus and continued looking at Uri, who seemed to be talking more to himself than to me. He was gazing at the ceiling and counting on his fingers. I had lost some of what he said, but I assumed he was still speaking about all the different options for the supposed ossuary of Mary Magdalene.

"There are so many different interpretations of the name," I chimed in, trying to appear as if I'd be listening the whole time.

Uri shifted his eyes down from the ceiling to me.

"Precisely," he said. "Mary, Maria, Mara, Mariamne, Mariamme, Mariam, Mariamnon...Every epigrapher asked to translate the ossuary has presented a different opinion. Some say there was one person in this ossuary. Others say there were two. As old as the inscriptions are, and as clumsily carved, there's not one shared interpretation among language experts."

"But among biblical scholars?" I asked. "Is there a general consensus among them about this ossuary?"

"Well, sure," Uri said. "Scholars believe there were two people interred in this bone box."

I was writing in my notebook when his next statement caught me off guard.

"And if there were two people contained in this ossuary," he said, "we can't even be sure if they were both female."

"What do you mean?" I asked. "Of course they're both female."

Uri wagged a finger at me, as if I should've known the answer to this latest puzzle. "There are nine known ossuaries that contain the name Mara, and in two of the cases it is believed the name Mara belonged to men."

"Men named Mara?" I said. "I didn't realize Mara is a unisex name."

"Well, it's not, exactly," Uri said, wrinkling his nose as if to suggest the answer was complicated. "Jewish names that could be used as both male and female are rare. The ossuaries we've seen with Mara etched on them were clearly indicating the Aramaic word for *master*."

"Mariamene and her master?" I said, translating into English yet another interpretation of the Mary Magdalene ossuary.

"Yes. The 'master' most likely being her husband."

"Of course," I said, rolling my eyes.

Uri shrugged, as if he was just stating the facts, that he shouldn't be blamed for the implication of female subservience.

"So the person interred with Mariamene, the Mara part of the inscription, could be a female relative...or her husband," I said, summarizing the two options for the second person interred in the ossuary.

"Yes, both very good possibilities," Uri said.

"That shoots a lot of holes in the Mary Magdalene theory," I said, writing down more notes. "And if this isn't the ossuary of Mary Magdalene, then the house of cards falls apart. It throws even more doubt on the claim that the Talpiot tomb is the final resting place of Jesus."

Uri inhaled deeply and opened his mouth like he was about to say something, and then stopped. "Let's move on," he said after a brief pause. "There is one last treasure to behold."

CHAPTER EIGHTEEN

"Close your eyes," Uri said.

"What?"

"Close your eyes."

We were standing in yet another aisle, surrounded by bone boxes stacked floor to ceiling on high metal shelves.

Uri reached out and took my right hand in his. My heart started to beat faster.

"Mara yakiri. B'vakasha," Uri said in Hebrew. *My dear Mara. Please.*

I closed my eyes.

"You are here to see, but also to feel," he said, gently lifting my hand until I felt cool stone on my fingertips.

"Sham," he said. *There.* "Do you feel that?"

As he guided my hand over the smooth surface I felt deep carved lines in the stone under my fingers.

"Yes, I feel it," I said. "Is that an inscription? Someone's name?"

"Achat, shtayim, shalosh, arba, hamesh, shesh," Uri whispered softly in my ear, counting off the number of letters as he traced them with my fingertips.

"Six letters," Uri said. "They spell Yeshua."

My eyes popped open. We were standing next to the controversial ossuary that started it all.

Yeshua bar Yosef.

Jesus son of Joseph.

I was touching what may be the vessel that contained the remains of Jesus Christ.

It was then that I noticed Uri was standing unbelievably close to me. Our feet were nearly touching and his hand still held mine. With a few more steps our lips would meet in a kiss.

For a moment I felt it: requited attraction. The way Uri whispered almost seductively in my ear. How close our bodies were. How tenderly he held my hand. There was a longing in his eyes, a curiosity I felt as he leaned in toward me. As if he was thinking, *What would it be like to kiss this American girl?*

How badly I wanted him to follow through. How palpable my desire to kiss this Israeli man... But not here. Not now.

I lowered my eyes and took a few steps back, forcing myself to temporarily ignore my feelings for Uri and attempt to keep this meeting strictly professional.

"Mara?" he asked, sensing my discomfort.

I fumbled with my notebook and cleared my throat. "So...this is it?" I asked, looking at the ossuary for the first time. "The supposed bone box of Jesus..."

Keep it together, I told myself. *Focus.*

I trained my eye on the ancient inscription, the one that indicated this ossuary may have contained the remains of the most controversial person the world has ever known. The inscription was located on the narrow side facing out, directly under the rim. The inscription was preceded by a mark that resembled an X or a cross tilted on one side. The ossuary itself was undecorated and badly scratched, its lid flat and broken. Hardly the type of vessel you'd think would contain the remains of Jesus of Nazareth.

Uri looked at me, his eyes flickering back and forth as if reading my thoughts. He smiled, then continued.

"Yes, so, this portion of the inscription is generally accepted to read Yeshua," he said, pointing to the clumsily carved letters immediately to the right of the cross mark. As he pointed I could see his hand trembling.

"Jesus," I translated. "A common name at the time, right?"

"The sixth most popular name," Uri said.

"And that part of the inscription?" I asked, pointing to the farthest left part of the etching.

"Bar Yehosef. Son of Joseph."

"I don't know anything about ancient languages, but even I can tell you that this inscription is very difficult to make out," I said, moving closer to the ossuary and squinting, as if doing so would make the scribbles legible. "It looks like it was inscribed by a child."

"Keep in mind, Mara, that inscriptions were usually made by family members of the dead, using crude instruments like chisels and nails, and often in the darkness of a tomb. So carelessly executed etchings, sometimes with misspelled words, were very common."

Uri seemed to have also regained his focus.

"But someone as important as Jesus of Nazareth?" I challenged Uri. "Certainly more care would have been taken for his ossuary."

"This is not surprising. Even ossuaries of renowned families and high-ranking officials are known to be illegible and contain spelling mistakes."

In an effort to assuage my disbelief, Uri mentioned again the common Jewish practice of second burial: A body is laid out to decompose, and then, about a year later, the remains are placed in an ossuary where they would remain forever in a family cave.

This is vastly different from the burial practices of modern Jerusalem, Uri said. Ossuaries would have been seen by family members only, shut away in dusty caves that only family members accessed, not put on display for the whole world to see.

I had to remember that Jesus was a simple man who had humble beginnings. The earliest "Christians," the ones who existed during Jesus' time, followed a Jewish brand of theology. To them, and to Jesus' family as well, Jesus was neither a God nor a deity, despite the importance placed on him by his disciples. Therefore, his family still adhered to Jewish burial practices when he died; a simple burial in a non-descript cave, and a simple bone box clumsily etched with his name to house his remains. It was modern Christianity that created pomp and circumstance for Jesus' sake: fabricated holidays to celebrate the supposed dates of his birth and death and resurrection; cavernous churches and highly embellished cathedrals in which to pray; and a long tradition of popes and bishops and cardinals and priests to keep us in line, to remind us to do as they say, not as they do.

The politics of religion aside, there was a bone box in front of me demanding my attention, an ossuary that a controversial documentary claimed was the final resting place of Jesus of Nazareth. I was beginning to have my doubts that this theory was real, but the fate of my novel depended on it. I couldn't allow myself to get wrapped up in the state of modern Christianity.

"I think you're missing something," I said to Uri after he had concluded his speech about Jewish burial practices.

"I am?" he said.

"The X mark," I said, looking again at the etching of what looked like a cross tilted on its side.

"Ah, yes," Uri said.

"Is it a Christian symbol of the cross? Is it meant to denote that someone important, like Jesus, is inside?"

"No, it is probably a mark of the stone mason or the person who etched the inscription." Uri pointed to a mark on the lid, this one looking like a greater-than sign. "Here's another example."

"So the fact that the X mark looks like a cross and just happens to be preceding the name Jesus is just coincidence?"

"I'm afraid so. X marks were typically used to show how the ossuary was supposed to align with the lid, and there would be two matching symbols, one of the box and one on the lid. There are many ossuaries at Dominus Flevit that prove this theory. In this case, and on a lot of the other ossuaries that have been discovered, the marks were used to identify the mason or inscriber."

"Not religious in nature," I summed up.

"It looks that way. Besides, the cross was not established as a Christian symbol until the time of Emperor Constantine, in the fourth century A.D."

"Surely the cross as symbol was used before then," I said. "Certainly the early Christians made the connection that Christ died on a cross and therefore a cross was the most powerful and enduring symbol they had to remember him by."

I was grasping at straws. The X mark as Christian symbol would be a strong argument in proving the validity of the Talpiot tomb. It was also one of the last pieces of evidence I had. Without it, the X mark was just another piece of graffiti, a stray mark among many on a stone box that I was using to tell the world that everything previously thought about Jesus' life was a lie. But as it stood now, the X was just another hole in my story.

"Perhaps the early Christians passed the history of the cross symbol along in oral traditions until it was finally adopted several hundred years later as the official symbol of Christianity," I was saying when Uri reached out and took my hand.

"I know you think you need this argument," he said, "but you'll have to find another way."

I looked at Uri, over to the box that had been causing me such frustration, and finally at the ground.

"Why?" I whispered.

"Crucifixion is something that no one should have to endure," Uri said, releasing my hand. "To the early Christians, the cross would have been a painful reminder that their son, their friend, their leader, had died a long, cruel and excruciating death. Why would they willingly subject themselves to such emotional torture by adopting a symbol that would be a constant reminder of that?"

"No, that's not what I meant when I asked why," I said.

Uri looked at me curiously.

I felt chastened, like this was a lost cause. There seemed to be no avenues left to explore. Everything could be explained away. Ancient stone boxes carved only with first names, and common names at that. Cross symbols that were little more than instructions for lid and box alignment. Bones that had been reburied nearly thirty years ago and long forgotten. With all evidence pointing to the Talpiot tomb not being the final resting place of Jesus, how could I possibly convince everyone that it was?

It was then I realized that I hadn't yet looked at the *Yehudah bar Yeshua* ossuary, the bone box that some believed belonged to Jesus' son, Jude. But what would be the point? If there was no strong evidence proving that the ossuaries belonged to Jesus and his family, then what difference would one more ossuary make? DNA testing couldn't even conclusively link the Jesus and Mariamene ossuaries, and there was no other evidence whatsoever of a marriage or proof of a child...

I didn't even want to look at the Yehuda ossuary. I didn't need another slap in the face, another reminder that my mission had failed, that I would be returning to Philadelphia empty-handed.

"Why is this so hard?" I asked, more of myself than Uri. But he answered anyway.

"Because you're one person attempting to challenge a two thousand year-old institution that is one billion people strong, nothing less than a religion that has formed the foundation of western civilization."

I leaned against a metal shelf. "I'm lost."

"How do you mean?" Uri asked.

"There's nothing left. How can I...how can I write this book? It wouldn't be right. None of it would be true. I'd be lying..."

"Make no mistake, Mara, this is the ossuary of Jesus," Uri stated authoritatively, standing up straight and pointing to the stone box sitting on a shelf next to us.

I sighed. Why was Uri trying to confuse me? He claimed he wanted me to draw my own conclusions about the Talpiot tomb. Which I had. I was pretty sure the Talpiot tomb did not belong to Jesus of Nazareth and his family. But with the right amount of spin I could novelize it and make the claim legitimate. If only I could stay in Jerusalem with Uri until I figured out how to do that...

So why was Uri now trying to lead me to a conclusion? Why was he stating the ossuary in front of us did belong to Jesus? I was lost and confused and hadn't the energy to continue our exploration.

"Uri," I said, "I'm tired."

Uri looked at me lovingly and took a few steps toward me. He leaned against me, the metal shelf now supporting both of our weights.

"I think you're...I mean, you must know how I..." I stammered, the words muffled by his shoulder as it pressed against my cheek. I was attempting to let Uri know that I appreciated everything he had done for me. No, that I would be nowhere without his help. But given my exhaustion and Uri's sudden advances, I couldn't begin to express it.

And there was no way in hell that I could even come close to saying what was really running through my mind at that moment: That I thought Uri was a remarkable man and I found myself falling uncontrollably for him.

Uri gently kissed my forehead. "There's no need," he said. "I understand."

"You do?" I asked.

Uri gave me a squeeze before stepping away from our embrace. "Let's go. We're done for the day."

"OK," I said. "So what's next?"

"We still have one thing left to see," Uri said. And then he leaned in close and whispered in my ear, "Tomorrow night we visit the tomb."

CHAPTER NINETEEN

I t was a cool night and the dark sky was full of stars. A light breeze
nipped at us as we walked, and I was glad I decided to wear a light
jacket. As we approached the clearing I saw him, standing alone with
his hands in his pockets, a large duffle bag at his feet.

"Hello, Miss Mara," he said as Uri and I walked towards him. It had
been a few days since I'd seen him, and it felt good to be greeted by a
friendly face.

Instinctively I hugged him, wrapping my arms around his thin
shoulders.

"Hi, Lev."

"It's been some time," he said. "I haven't seen you in the store lately."

"I'm sorry. I...well..." I started to explain.

"It's okay. I understand," Lev said, looking at me and then to Uri.
"You've been busy."

There was a moment of silence between the three of us, and I
wondered what Lev was thinking. I looked over at Uri for some sign
as to what the quiet meant, but he seemed to be lost in his own world,
staring at the entrance to the tomb, which I noticed was uncovered.
The stone slab that had been welded in place was now laying askew
across the stone walls that had been built to box out the entrance to the
tomb.

"Did you do that?" I asked Lev, pointing to the unobstructed
entrance just a few steps away.

"I had help," he said.

"How did you...?" I asked. "Who...?"

"Does it really matter, Miss Mara? It is done. It is time for you to do
what you've most been wanting to do. Your whole reason for coming to
Jerusalem." He reached into the duffel bag and pulled out a rope ladder.
"Here. You will need this to get down to the entrance of the tomb."

I looked at Lev and then at Uri, the two men now exchanging glances.

"You're not coming with us?" I asked Lev.

"Someone must stand guard," he said.

I looked around at the large apartment buildings around us, their lower levels shrouded by trees and shrubbery. Talpiot was a popular residential suburb of Jerusalem, notable for its clubs and restaurants and for the tomb discovered during the construction of the apartment complex nearly thirty years before. A tomb that a controversial documentary claimed was the final resting place of Jesus of Nazareth, a tomb I had come thousands of miles to see, and would be inside in a matter of minutes.

A dog barked off in the distance, but otherwise all was still and quiet.

Uri gently took hold of my elbow, leading me up the small stone steps toward the entrance of the tomb.

I motioned to Lev. "Are you sure you can't come with us?"

"Too risky," he whispered. "There isn't much time and you'll need a lookout."

Uri unrolled the rope ladder, secured it to one of the concrete walls that boxed out the entrance to the tomb, and instructed me to go first. He shined a flashlight down the shaft and I hoisted myself over the wall and slowly down the ladder. Thousand-year-old dirt crunched beneath my shoes as I hit the bottom and stepped out of the way to make room for Uri's descent. He climbed down, unsteadily at first, his left hand bearing all the weight as his right hand held the flashlight.

"First thing's first," Uri said, shining the flashlight on the area just above the tomb entrance. I turned around to see what he was motioning to. There, etched deeply into the rock, was what looked like an upside-down letter V with a circle in the middle of it.

"I've seen that symbol before," I said.

"A circle, or rosette, under a gable," Uri explained. "You probably remember it from Dominus Flevit. Some of the ossuaries kept there have this symbol etched on them. Do you remember me showing them to you?"

"Yes, I remember. One of the ossuaries, etched with the name Simon bar Jonah, had this symbol etched on it."

"Peter, son of Jonah," Uri translated from Hebrew. "Yes, the dot and gable symbol on that ossuary are quite unmistakable."

"I've read that some people actually believe that ossuary belongs to the apostle Peter. As in, the great Saint Peter! Can you imagine?"

"Don't you think that's possible?"

"That his remains are stored in a plain ossuary in Jerusalem rather than a necropolis under the basilica in Rome that bears his name?"

"Yes."

"I don't know. Tradition says his remains are in Rome."

"Ah, tradition," Uri said. "Such a tricky word when science is involved. Tradition would also have you believe that Jesus was resurrected on the site of what is now the Church of the Holy Sepulchre. Aren't we here to prove the opposite? That he in fact did not resurrect, that his body lied right here in this tomb, miles from Jerusalem, for nearly two thousand years?"

"Yes, but this is different," I said.

"How so?"

"Because there is no mention of Peter being resurrected from the dead. He was martyred for his beliefs and his remains were buried...somewhere. It doesn't really matter where. Could be Rome. Could be Jerusalem."

"So you've seen the gable symbol etched on an ossuary and now on this tomb," Uri said, shifting the focus of our conversation back to the symbol above the entrance to the tomb. "What do you think it means?"

"Some Christian symbol, maybe?"

"At first glance, one would think it is. The Dominus Flevit chapel, after all, was built on the site where Christians believed Jesus of Nazareth sat and mourned the fate of Jerusalem. Since the chapel has a long Christian history, it's easy to see how the circle and gable found on many of the ossuaries there could be misinterpreted as being a Christian symbol."

"Misinterpreted?"

"This symbol is common in ancient Jewish art and architecture," Uri explained. "It can be seen in synagogues in Palestine and elsewhere around the world, and in catacombs and tombs that are of Jewish descent. Tombs excavated at Beth Shearim in Galilee, for example, were found to have similar gable motifs. All of this art and architecture pre-dates Christianity."

"The symbol is pre-Christian, has nothing to do with Jesus and his movement, and is therefore strictly Jewish," I concluded.

"That's right."

"So what does the symbol represent?"

"It's most likely a reference to the Second Temple. A lot of the artifacts that contain a gable and rosette have been dated to the time of Herod the Great, who was responsible for the reconstruction of the Second Temple. It was during his reign that Jesus of Nazareth was born."

"Hence another reason why people would incorrectly identify the gable as a Christian symbol: because it was a popular motif during Jesus' time."

"Exactly," Uri said, taking a step closer to the tomb entrance. "Now, enough about that. We mustn't wait another minute. Are you ready?"

I nodded.

"Good. Let's finally see what brought you to Jerusalem."

CHAPTER TWENTY

"Welcome to the tomb, the final resting place, of Jesus," he said. Uri had just shone his flashlight into the six loculi that radiated out like spokes on a wheel from the inner chamber of the tomb, where we now found ourselves crouched on our knees, breathing in the dusty air. These six deep niches were empty, their contents now resting in various museums around Jerusalem. But I imagined how the ossuaries had been positioned inside the loculi, recalling from photocopies I had seen of sketches made during the time of the original tomb excavation.

The most important ossuary, at least in my mind—the *Yeshua bar Yohosef* ossuary—had been found in the loculi closest to the tomb entrance on the eastern wall. As Uri's flashlight beam came to rest inside this deep niche, I saw the Jesus son of Joseph inscription in my mind, on the narrow side of the ossuary under the rim, badly scratched and clumsily carved, like graffiti on a concrete wall.

"The final resting place of Jesus of Nazareth, huh?" I asked. I inspected Uri's face in the dim light. "Do you truly believe that?"

"Given more research, more testing..." he said, and then, after a moment, "Who knows?"

"So you don't believe this is the tomb of Jesus? I thought you said..." I trailed off, suddenly unsure of what, exactly, Uri had said he believed.

"Make no mistake, Mara. This is the tomb of Jesus. A Jesus who lived and worked in Jerusalem in the first century A.D. Perhaps it is Jesus Christ, perhaps not. I never said I believed anything otherwise."

"So why did you let me believe that this could be the tomb of the holy family?"

Uri sighed and looked at me empathetically. "I'm sorry if you feel deceived. But you led yourself to your own conclusions. I only told you what I knew and showed you the artifacts. The rest was up to you."

I thought about his comment a minute. "I suppose you're right."

Uri moved closer and took my hand. "You told me several days ago at the warehouse in Beth Shemesh that you didn't think you could write the book because you didn't believe. That it was all a lie and you didn't feel right telling the whole world this tomb belonged to Jesus Christ. You came to that conclusion before you even knew what I thought."

"Yes, I did say that," I said, looking at Uri's hand as it caressed the top of mine. I had grown used to the way that felt, how he wrapped his palm around my fingers and gently kneaded the skin. Within the past week or so, Uri started to do it with more frequency, reach out and, without notice or warning, grasp my hand. I felt comforted by it, welcomed it, even, like a soft blanket around the shoulders on a cold night. And after our experience at the Beth Shemesh warehouse, where I all but backed away from his kiss, I think holding my hand was Uri's way of showing he could be respectfully affectionate without overtly breaching the line of professionalism he thought I wanted to maintain.

If he only knew...

"So there's nothing left for us to discuss," I said, awakening from my reverie to the realization that my legs were starting go numb from the way I was kneeling with my feet pinned beneath me. Uri was in a crouched position, his arms resting on his bent knees.

"Actually, there is," Uri said, releasing my hand as I shifted positions and sat cross-legged. "There is still one more piece of the puzzle. Perhaps the most important piece. If there is to be any truth to the theory of the Talpiot tomb, then we must reconcile what we know with this last piece of the puzzle. A piece that is absolutely crucial to the Christian faith."

I thought a moment, pouring over everything Uri and I had discussed over the past few weeks: The names on the ossuaries; the historic sites of Jesus' sermons and appearances; his birth in Bethlehem; his life in Jerusalem; the possibility of his marriage to Mary Magdalene and raising a child named Judah; his death at the hands of the Roman authorities; the traditional site of his...

"Resurrection!" I called out. "We've never discussed his resurrection!"

"Yes, that's it exactly," Uri said. "If there is to be any truth to what is being said about the Talpiot tomb, then we must reconcile the Christian belief in resurrection with the existence of the Jesus bone box."

"Why is resurrection such a large piece of the puzzle?"

"Because a lot hinges on the definition of resurrection."

"The *definition*...?"

"If you stick with the New Testament accounts of the resurrection, then Jesus' tomb was found empty shortly after the resurrection," Uri explained.

"Right. So?"

"So, that is in line with the predominant Jewish notion of the afterlife at the time—that of bodily resurrection."

"So the traditional definition of resurrection is ascending body and soul into heaven."

"Correct."

"So if Jews in first century Palestine believed in bodily resurrection, then there should be no Jesus bone box, because his family and disciples would've expected him to be resurrected and therefore not require an ossuary," I recapped.

"It seems that way," Uri said. "And Jesus' disciples claimed to have seen the risen Jesus on several occasions. This would suggest a bodily resurrection, which would explain why Mary Magdalene, the Mother Mary, and others, according to the New Testament, witnessed an empty tomb. All ancient sources, in fact, point to an empty tomb. Even Jewish authorities at the time thought his tomb was empty."

I didn't like how this conversation was going. I thought Uri said the resurrection theory was supposed to help my case? It seemed to be making things worse. I thought about approaching the resurrection debate from a different angle.

"If Jesus hadn't been resurrected," I said, "do you think the disciples had reason to lie and say he did?"

"Not a chance," Uri said, shaking his head. "They would risk ridicule and possible death for lying. Most of them were eventually martyred for their belief in Jesus, but why risk being martyred for a lie? To suggest they would do so is ludicrous."

That made sense, but again, it did little to help prove the Talpiot tomb was real.

"Most scholars conclude that the disciples truly believed they had seen a risen Jesus," Uri said. "Their account in the New Testament and a lack of other explanations or alternatives leads us to believe the disciples were telling the truth. Not exactly what you want to hear, Mara, but interesting nonetheless."

"Well, there is, in fact, another explanation for sightings of a resurrected Jesus."

Uri raised an eyebrow.

"We must remain open to the fact that the Bible is fiction," I began. "And that every person in the Bible is a character within a made-up story."

"That might very well be your belief," Uri said, "but for our purposes it's best to assume the Bible is a historical record of real people."

"C'mon, Uri. An ark with two of every animal on it? Burning bushes that speak? Men that live to be hundreds of years old...?"

"The Bible is one of the few resources we have." And then he was silent, and I heard nothing inside the tomb except the echo of his words.

I have offended him, I thought. Uri was a scholarly man, an educated man of science who sought out the truth at all costs. But he was still Jewish, and I had questioned the validity of his faith and the existence of his ancestors.

"I'm sorry, Uri. I was out of line," I said. "It's just that I thought you said the resurrection theory was supposed to help my case. But it seems to be the final nail in the coffin."

"How so?"

"Well, for instance, if Jesus was resurrected, how do you explain the New Testament account of Mary Magdalene and the Mother Mary going to his tomb to prepare his body for burial? Wouldn't they have anticipated resurrection? And if so, why did they seem so surprised to find an empty tomb?"

"You think that because they went to visit his tomb they weren't anticipating the resurrection, and maybe therefore didn't believe in resurrection?"

"I guess what I'm saying is, if Mary Magdalene and the Mother Mary prepared his body for burial, what does that say about their faith? Since they were Jewish, then they should have believed in reincarnation. That is, body and soul. So Jesus' body shouldn't have been there."

"Now you see why resurrection is such a crucial piece of the puzzle," Uri said. "It's such a complicated subject."

"Right, because it's not just limited to Mary Magdalene and the Mother Mary," I continued. "Think of all the people listed in the New Testament who claim to have seen a resurrected Jesus: Peter, Paul, Jesus' own brother James...they are some of the most important disciples. What does it say about them if they believed in Jesus' resurrection while simultaneously accepting an ossuary with Jesus' name on it? Given the presence of a body and an ossuary to house his bones, how could Jesus' disciples go on believing that he had truly risen from the dead?"

"You make a good point, Mara. Knowing the truth about what happened to Jesus' body, how could anyone's faith remain unchanged?"

"That is the heart of it, isn't it?" I asked. "If Jesus' disciples believed in bodily resurrection, but then they heard about his body being prepared after death and were witness to an ossuary that would house his bones, how could they possibly go on believing that Jesus was the son of God?"

"Yes, my dear Mara," Uri said. "We have reached the very heart of the conflict. And there is no evidence that the disciples didn't believe in the resurrection, and the fact that they were willing to die for their beliefs is telling."

"Not exactly what I wanted to hear, Uri," I said.

"That is why we must present another alternative to the resurrection theory," he said.

"Another theory..." I said, sighing. I wasn't sure I could stomach another theory. My mind was already swimming, the tomb was stifling, and the stale, dusty air was starting to wreak havoc on my lungs.

"The disciples' faith would remain unchanged if we were to change the definition of resurrection," Uri explained.

"The definition of resurrection..." I whispered. This was how our whole conversation started, with Uri stating that resurrection was central to Christian origins. But that it depended on your *definition* of resurrection...

"Think about it," Uri said, shifting positions so that he was now also sitting cross-legged. "The resurrection of Jesus is the main event that affirms the validity of Christianity, right?"

"Right."

"And even Jesus himself said his resurrection would prove that he was the true son of God. But the Bible doesn't give a good indication of what resurrection means. Up to this point we've only been discussing a *bodily* resurrection."

"What are you getting at?"

Uri smiled and paused a moment. "How about a *spiritual* resurrection?"

"Spiritual resurrection," I repeated. "As in, your spirit, or soul, rises to heaven but your physical body is left behind? Isn't that what a lot of other world religions are based on?"

"Yes, of course."

"But the New Testament doesn't exactly allow that as an option, does it?"

"Not really. But I think spiritual resurrection is a possible option, and it would certainly help your case."

"How?"

"In order to prove that the Talpiot tomb is real, we must somehow reconcile Jesus' resurrection with the discovery of an ossuary that contains his bones. Spiritual resurrection allows you to do that."

"Meaning a bodily resurrection, partnered with an ossuary containing his remains, would essentially falsify Christianity. But a spiritual resurrection and an ossuary have little impact because it wouldn't affect anyone's faith."

Uri nodded.

"But is that what the Apostles meant when they said they saw Jesus rise from the dead?"

"Well, yes and no," Uri said. "The New Testament gospels make it clear that Jesus' tomb was empty, and that his corpse, through bodily resurrection, was made immortal. But the apostle Paul...he's a different story."

"Why?"

"The term 'spiritual' appears many times in the New Testament, but the majority of these occurrences appear in Paul's writings. In Paul's letter to the Corinthians, for example, he talks about spiritual blessings, spiritual wisdom, spiritual gifts, spiritual songs..."

"Wow, Paul was quite a spiritual guy," I joked.

Uri laughed. "Well, it indicates that Paul possibly believed humans could be either natural or spiritual. In other words, they existed in a mortal, physical body, or as an immortal spirit powered by God."

"But Paul is just one apostle among many. How could he be the only one willing to accept the spiritual resurrection of Jesus while most others still believed in bodily resurrection?"

"Yes, that's true," Uri conceded. "But keep in mind that Paul is the earliest known author to discuss the resurrection of Jesus. Most scholars believe that the gospels were written after Paul had ministered, written his letters, and been martyred."

"What does that prove?"

"It proves that since Paul was one of the first people to discuss resurrection, his views carried a lot of weight and must've been influential. Furthermore, there's no doubt Paul knew the other apostles. So if he did believe in spiritual resurrection, certainly the other apostles knew he was preaching that message, and might've even approved his gospel. Meaning, the spiritual resurrection of Jesus might've been accepted by the other apostles."

"So if the other apostles accepted the spiritual resurrection of Jesus, a message that Paul had been preaching all along, then it's possible that the other gospels written after Paul's death were heavily influenced by Paul. The gospel writers could very well have modified their own view of resurrection and adopted Paul's theory of spiritual resurrection."

"Yes, Mara. That's it exactly," Uri said. "Spiritual resurrection would save Christianity, this tomb...and your novel."

"So the Talpiot tomb could very well be the final resting place of Jesus of Nazareth, after all?"

"Yes, my dear Mara. There's hope for this tomb yet. And hope for—"

Uri stopped mid-sentence and whipped his head toward the tomb entrance.

"What?" I asked.

"I thought I heard someone," he whispered.

The tomb was quiet, and if not for the raspy sound of my lungs struggling for fresh air, I might have been able to hear a spider scurrying across the dirt floor.

Suddenly I heard a voice echoing down from above. Uri must have heard it too because he hurriedly crawled to the entrance and stood at the bottom of the rope ladder, listening. I rushed after him, grabbing the flashlight he had left behind on my way out. A cloud of dust had followed us out of the tomb, and as it hit my nostrils I sputtered and coughed.

A voice made way its way down the hole to us, the same voice as before, this time a higher pitch, more anxious.

"Lev?" Uri called out.

Lev appeared at the entrance to the tomb. Uri took the flashlight from me and shined it up toward him, at the scared, wide-eyed face that betrayed our fate.

"Uri! Mara!" he yelled down to us. "You must get out now! They are coming!"

"Who's coming?" I yelled up to Lev.

"Lev...?" Uri asked.

Uri and Lev exchanged a glance.

Uri motioned to me. "Up the ladder, quickly!"

"What's going on?" I asked.

"No time for questions," Uri said, not waiting for me to reach the top before climbing up the ladder behind me.

"I don't understand!" I said, frantically clasping at each rung of the ladder as my feet struggled to carry me to safety.

By the time I reached the top of the rope ladder and white hot floodlights blinded me, I understood. I was not, in fact, climbing to safety. I was ascending to hell.

The bright floodlights burned my eyes as I scurried over the concrete wall and shuffled over to where I thought Lev stood. I blinked repeatedly, unable to find Lev, and unsure if Uri had made it to the top of the rope ladder.

"Lev? Uri?" I called out. "Where are you?"

"Miss Mara Beltane?" said a gruff male voice. He stood just in front of me.

"Yes? Who are you?"

"Miss Beltane, you and your friends must come with me."

The man took hold of my arm and pulled me toward the blinding white lights, which turned out to be the headlights of his police car. He placed me in the back of the car next to Lev, who was shivering, his head lowered.

My door slammed shut and a man climbed behind the wheel. The engine purred to life and our vehicle peeled away into the night. I twisted in my seat. Through the dust-strewn rear windshield I saw Uri being ushered into the back seat of a second Israeli police car.

That is the last image I saw before finally closing my eyes and wishing it was all a dream.

CHAPTER TWENTY-ONE

I was sitting in a prison cell in the District Headquarters of the Israeli Police Force in Jerusalem. I was alone in the cell, and Lev was in his own cell next to mine. There were only bars for walls, so I was able to look over and see him sitting on the concrete floor, his legs pulled to his chest. He hadn't said a word to me since we first met at the entrance of the tomb, about two hours before.

"Lev, are you alright?" I asked.

He nodded.

Just then Uri and two police escorts rounded the corner and walked down the hall in our direction. It was the first time I had seen Uri since he was placed into the back of a police car. He looked tired and paler than normal.

The cell to my immediate right was empty. One of the escorts unlocked it and Uri stepped inside. The cell was locked again and the two escorts wordlessly walked away. Uri sat on the wooden bench in his cell and eyed me wearily. For perhaps the first time I didn't have anything to say to him, so I offered a weak smile instead.

"Uri...?" Lev called out.

"Everything's fine, Lev," Uri said. "Just as we expected."

"What do you mean, Uri?" I asked, walking over to the wall of bars that separated us. "Are we going to be arrested?"

"No."

"Were you interrogated?" I asked.

"I was asked a lot of questions," Uri said. He looked past me to Lev. "And he was very thorough."

"Who?" I asked, looking over at Lev.

"My brother-in-law," Lev said.

"You mean Benjamin Schwarz, the head of the Jerusalem district of the Israel Police?" I asked, and Lev nodded. "He was the person following me..."

"He was following all of us, Mara," Uri said.

"Both of you knew he was following us and neither of you told me?" I asked.

I looked from Uri to Lev, waiting for one of them to explain.

It was Uri who spoke.

"Mara, we didn't want to frighten you or derail your plans. We thought if you knew the truth you might call off the whole thing. And then you never would've accomplished your goal."

"And there was no way of knowing that my—" Lev said but then stopped himself, his attention diverted by something he saw down the hallway. Lev jumped to his feet as a man approached our cells.

It was Benjamin Schwarz. He looked different without his sunglasses, friendlier almost. I imagined his eyes would be dark and beady, making him appear evil, but as he approached our cells I saw that they were in fact large and blue and appealing in a trustworthy way.

"Uri," Benjamin said, nodding at him.

"Is anyone going to tell me what the hell's going on?" I asked, looking for answers from anyone, but eyeing Benjamin accusingly.

"Miss Beltane," Benjamin said. "I'm very sorry for detaining you and your friends. We just need to finish some paperwork and then we'll get you out of here." His voice was soft and soothing, not at all like the vicious bark I had anticipated.

"If we're not being arrested, then why put us in cells?"

"It was the only way we could ensure that you wouldn't flee," he explained. "Nothing personal, just standard protocol."

I wanted to hate him.

"You chased me through the streets of Jerusalem," I said. "You've been following all of us. You crank called me and Uri."

"But I never threatened any of you. And I never made contact."

"How did you even know what we were planning to do?" As the words came out, I knew. The common denominator, the tie that bound the three men. "Ziva."

Benjamin was straight-faced and Uri flinched at the sound of her name.

"Ziva told you about our plan, didn't she?" I said.

"Miss Beltane," Benjamin said calmly, "we received a call tonight about suspicious behavior in the Talpiot area of the city. We were obligated to respond."

"That only explains tonight. It doesn't explain why you've been following all of us."

"I admit to keeping an eye on you," Benjamin admitted. "But only because of a tip I received about illegal activity that you might be involved in."

He acted as if Ziva wasn't the source of the tip, the reason why we were all sitting in jail. If only Uri hadn't said anything to her, if only they didn't communicate at all. If only Benjamin and Lev didn't both love her, then they could admit that Ziva was the reason why our plan fell apart.

"My surveillance skills are obviously a little rusty," Benjamin said. "It appears I was hidden within your plain view. You noticed me right away."

I wanted to hate Benjamin Schwarz. But what he said made sense. He had never threatened me or accused me of anything. And neither Uri nor Lev said they were threatened either. Just that they were being followed. Given their past, their previous break-in of the Talpiot tomb, it's not surprising that the police would keep a close watch on them. Plus, what Uri, Lev and I had done was illegal; Benjamin could have easily arrested all three of us and he didn't. He decided to have mercy on us. But why?

I wanted to hate Benjamin Schwarz, but I couldn't.

"We'll have you out in a few minutes," Benjamin reiterated. He nodded at Uri, and then stepped in front of my cell. "Goodbye, Miss Beltane, and good luck. I hope you found what you were looking for."

"Thank you," I said.

Benjamin paused at Lev's cell. The two men eyed each other.

"Young man," Benjamin said, reaching through the bars and shaking his hand. "Take care. I'll see you soon."

"Bye, Ben."

When Benjamin was out of sight, Uri retreated to the bench in his cell and sat down heavily with a sigh.

"I'm so sorry," he said. "I hope you'll both forgive me."

"For what?" Lev asked. "Everything went according to plan."

"Wait..." I said. "What plan?"

"None of this is your fault," Lev continued. "We both went into this willingly. Right, Mara?"

"Uh, right," I said, distracted by Lev's mention of a plan that I was unaware of. "And Uri, there was no way you could have known Ziva would tell Benjamin."

Lev peered through the bars of his cell at Uri. "I hope you realize that I said nothing to my sister, not the first time and not this time," he said.

"It's okay," Uri said. "I believe you. I trusted her..."

"She betrayed all of us," I whispered under my breath. But Uri heard.

"Ziva tried to warn me," he said.

"She broke off your engagement and then turned around and married Benjamin. She broke your heart, and then she ratted you out to police. Twice."

Neither Uri nor Lev spoke.

"How can both of you so easily defend her! Lev, she betrayed you, too! Her own brother!"

"I don't agree with a lot of her decisions, Mara. We didn't speak for a long time after the incident. But she is my sister, so in time I will forgive her."

"I wish I could be as forgiving," I mumbled.

"Perhaps if you heard the whole story you might think differently of my sister," Lev said. "Uri, I think it's time Mara knows the whole truth."

"Can someone tell me what's going on?" I pleaded, leaning heavily against the wall, tired and confused.

"Ziva used to work for the IAA, at the Beth Shemesh warehouse where the six inscribed Talpiot tomb ossuaries are kept..." Uri began, shifting positions on the bench so that he was facing me.

"Wait, does this story involve the plan Lev was talking about?" I asked.

"He'll get to that," Lev said.

Uri continued.

"Ziva told me about the Talpiot tomb and the ossuaries when we first met. She took me to the warehouse and showed me the ossuaries. Naturally I was interested in their history. I thought it would make for a lively debate for my students.

"I joked with Ziva that I would break into the Talpiot tomb and prove it was the true resting place of Jesus of Nazareth. I was kidding, at first..."

"But Ziva took you seriously?" I asked.

"No, not at first. But the more research I did, the more I talked about the tomb and the ossuaries, the more anxious Ziva became. She accused me of being obsessed with the tomb. She warned me that talking about it with my students could jeopardize her job. And possibly mine. She begged me to let it go and not talk about it anymore."

"Did you?" I asked.

"For awhile. I asked Ziva to marry me. She said yes, and the majority of our conversations from then on were about the wedding. We no longer spoke about the Talpiot tomb. Ziva was happy, and so was I, but the Talpiot tomb was still there, in the back of my mind, beckoning to me..."

"What did you do?" I asked.

"I asked Ziva to use her power to convince the IAA to open the tomb for further investigation."

"And Ziva agreed to do that?"

"On one condition: That I would never talk about the Talpiot tomb in public again."

"Finding out the truth about the Talpiot tomb is your passion. How could she ask that of you?"

"At the time I believed it was fair," Uri explained. "I asked her to make a big sacrifice, and she asked for one in return."

"So what happened?"

"My request was denied, of course. I think we both knew it would be. Soon after, Ziva left."

"Just like that?" I said. "She left you for a stranger?"

"Ziva and Benjamin were hardly strangers," Uri said. "They'd known each other for several years. The IAA frequently works with the Jerusalem police to prevent theft, looting and other crimes against antiquities."

"So you wanted Ziva to ask the IAA powers-that-be to contemplate opening the Talpiot tomb for further investigation. Where's the sacrifice in that?"

"In the months leading up to my request, Ziva and Benjamin grew closer. She talked about him a lot. She spent a lot of time on cases with him. Late-night meetings. Early morning phone calls. I felt her pulling away from me...She was falling for Benjamin."

"Was she cheating on you?" I asked.

"She claims no. And I have to believe her. And that is where the big sacrifices came into play. I told her I'd give up the Talpiot tomb, stop talking about it, quit my research, if she would give up Benjamin and be with me."

I wanted to abhor Ziva Feldman. For breaking Uri's heart. For betraying Lev, her own flesh and blood. For snitching on us. I really wanted to hate her...

"Neither of those things happened, did they?" I asked.

"She didn't love me enough to stay," Uri said. "And we both knew I wouldn't be able to give up the Talpiot tomb. Neither of us could be trusted to live up to our word. So we went our separate ways. It seemed the only just thing to do. As you know, we remained friends..."

"A friendship she then betrayed by diming you out to her new husband," I said, "who just happens to be with the Jerusalem police."

"She was trying to protect me," Uri said. "She thought that if she told Benjamin about what I might be planning to do, then he would take it easy on me as a favor to her."

"She was trying to protect *herself*!" I said. "She wanted to keep her job and protect her reputation."

"The Talpiot tomb is public knowledge," Lev said. "Everyone knows where it is and where the ossuaries are kept. It's not a secret. And anyone can visit the Beth Shemesh warehouse. We didn't need any information from Ziva for our research or planning."

"Well, so much for Ziva's persuasion," I said. "Benjamin wound up arresting the both of you anyway!"

Uri and Lev looked at each other.

"We broke the law, plain and simple," Uri said. "Benjamin was only doing his job. It didn't matter that Benjamin is Ziva's husband. He had to uphold the law. No amount of pleading or persuasion on her part could've helped us. I don't blame him."

"Ziva tried to help, but in the end, we got caught," Lev added. "We might've gotten away with it had Ziva not told Benjamin, but probably not."

"Ziva felt responsible for what happened to the both of us," Uri said. "She resigned from the IAA because she didn't think it was fair that she got to keep her job and I didn't. Eventually she found a job at Hebrew University, which I helped her get."

I wanted to hate Ziva Feldman. I kept trying. But Uri and Lev would never allow it.

"How come Benjamin arrested you the last time despite Ziva's pleadings," I said, "but this time he was willing to let you go?"

"Ziva didn't tell Benjamin about our plan this time," Lev said. "I did."

I wanted to reach through the bars and shake him. "Why would you do that?"

"Ben is my brother-in-law," Lev said. "We have grown close. I thought if I explained to him how important seeing the Talpiot tomb was to the three of us, that I could work out a deal with him."

"So you told the police we were going to do something illegal, and then tried to negotiate a deal for us to get away with it?" I was flabbergasted.

"I thought it was worth a try," Lev said.

"What kind of deal did you work out?"

"I told Ben that if he helped us gain access to the tomb, that I'd agree to be in the Civilian Guard."

"Civilian Guard?" I asked, wondering how that worked into Lev's plan.

"The Civilian Guard is a group of local volunteers who help the police prevent crime," Uri explained. "These volunteers identify problems in their neighborhoods and single out what is required of the population in order for them to stay safe. The volunteers network with watch groups and the police to improve the quality of life for the inhabitants."

"You agreed to do that for us?" I asked Lev.

"Yes," Lev said. "My father, and Benjamin too, have been trying to convince me to join. I thought it would look good on my resume, so I decided to use it as leverage. A bargaining chip, you might say."

"And Benjamin agreed to this deal you came up with, knowing that he'd be helping us break the law?" I asked.

"It's only considered breaking the law if you get *caught*," Lev said slyly, a smirk on his face. "But in this case, the police already knew about it…"

"I don't understand," I said.

"The tomb sits on land that is owned by the Talpiot Apartment Owners' Association," Lev said. "If we were to gain access to the tomb, as civilians we could be charged with trespassing and breaking and entering and a whole bunch of other possible charges. But if the police are there, escorting us on 'official police business'…"

"But the police weren't there. It was just the three of us."

"Ben was there," Lev said. "As well as one of his field officers. Both of them were hiding in the bushes. Ben agreed to give us a thirty-minute head start. If we were still there after a half hour, he and his officer were going to come out and take us into custody. He agreed to not arrest us, however."

"Was not being arrested another stipulation of your deal?" I asked Lev.

"That part was Uri's idea," Lev said.

"Benjamin said that no matter what happened tonight, the incident couldn't go unrecorded," Uri said. "He'd have to give an explanation as to why he and his officer were at the Talpiot tomb. I agreed to give a written statement that said, in effect, I went to the Talpiot tomb to look at the exterior of it, and nothing else. When I arrived, there were some people hanging around, acting suspicious, so I called the police. It was dark, so I couldn't identify anyone. When the police arrived, the people ran off."

All of my questions had been answered and, it seemed, Uri's and Lev's story had ended. There was silence between the three of us, and I contemplated everything that had transpired.

Finally, I spoke.

"Uri, why were you willing to take the fall?"

"I didn't want you to get wrapped up in our plan, just in case something went wrong," he said. "I couldn't bear the thought of you getting in trouble."

Just then, the same two police escorts that had walked Uri back to his cell came around the corner. One of them had a set of keys in his hands. We were being released.

As the three of us made our way to the lobby, Uri said, "Now you understand the full implications of the Talpiot tomb, Mara. What some people are willing to do to protect it."

"The religious implications alone..." Lev said.

Uri nodded. "Allegations that the Talpiot tomb is the final resting place of Jesus of Nazareth is a slight against Christianity and everything they believe and stand for."

"But it's not even true," I said. "At least, it hasn't been proven yet."

"The fact that a dialogue even exists is considered blasphemy," Uri said.

Tovah's comment during my tour of the Rockefeller Museum made sense now: *Israel has seen enough war and terror and doesn't need another battle on its hands.*

The Bible is, according to Christian tradition, still the best existing historical record of Jesus' life. It references his death on the cross. It mentions resurrection and ghostly sightings of Jesus after his death. But it doesn't say he was married. It doesn't say he fathered children. And the Bible certainly doesn't say that he left behind a pile of bones in a stone box stored in a family tomb.

Spiritual resurrection was my last hope of proving the Talpiot tomb's validity, but most Christians don't believe that is a possibility. They believe in bodily resurrection—no body left behind. So if any of that other stuff proved valid—a wife, some kids, a tomb? It could mean World War III. It leant credence to Uri's comment to his student, who asked about the possibility of a Jesus/Mary Magdalene marriage: *We may never know. We may never be allowed to know.*

Uri, Lev and I walked out the front door of the police station into the cool night air. I was silent for a minute, allowing my thoughts to sink in, deciding my next move.

"Now what, Miss Mara?" Lev asked.

"Now, I go home."

CHAPTER TWENTY-TWO

The old Mercedes eased through traffic without much trouble. It was early Saturday morning, and the streets and sidewalks of the New City were nearly deserted in observance of the Sabbath. Uri had a look of constrained intensity on his face as he drove that could have easily been mistaken for the focus needed to navigate the normally traffic-choked streets. But there were no distractions to speak of: no traffic jams or broken-down cars blocking traffic or pedestrians darting into the street. And yet there it was—a furrow of the brow that contorted his face ever so slightly.

Uri's face must be betraying some other emotion, then, and one I had seen only moments before.

"Is everything all right?" I asked as we continued to drive west, now on the outskirts of town.

He gave me a weary smile. "Of course."

"I appreciate the ride to the airport. I know it is an inconvenience for you today"

"It is no inconvenience."

"Did I tell you how grateful I am for everything you've done for me?"

The intense look dissipated ever so briefly into another weary smile. "More than enough times. It was my pleasure, Mara." The brow furrowed again. "But you didn't accomplish your mission."

"My mission...?"

"Your novel."

"I could still write the novel." I thought a moment. "But it's probably not meant to be."

I realized that statement, in light of a recent impulsive act, had suddenly taken on new meaning. The thought of my brash move, the embarrassment I now felt, caused me to look away, out the window at the dusty landscape. I didn't want Uri to see the sudden blush that had arisen in my cheeks.

"I feel responsible," he said.

I continued watching the city disappear and the dry sands of the Jerusalem suburbs emerge.

"For what?" I asked.

"For leading you on a wild-goose chase."

"It wasn't a wild-good chase. It was an adventure and learning experience for me."

We glanced at each other and he noticed me playing with the edges of the envelope I held in my lap.

"So you don't regret coming to Jerusalem?" he asked.

"Oh, Uri. I will never regret this trip. I honestly don't know what I would've done without you."

He looked at me then and our eyes met briefly and I stopped myself from continuing. I was dangerously close to spurting out my feelings for Uri, something I promised myself I wouldn't do again because feelings—however deep or sincere—could never change our circumstances.

But at least a near verbal slip was easier to recover from. My first offense, which had occurred only about twenty minutes before in the doorway of my hotel room, would prove harder to forget.

I had opened my hotel room door and saw Uri's handsome face and I threw myself into his arms and kissed him.

It wasn't something I had planned to do, it just...happened. I heard a soft knock, I opened the door, and there he was, prepared to take me to the airport. He was glad to be able to see me one last time but sad to see me go, and he said as much, but with an intensity on his face that suggested he didn't quite know how to express it.

But I did. In that split second I knew how to express my own feelings and emotions, and I hoped that a kiss would allow him to let go, to finally give in to his emotions, too. It could be our last chance, I thought. We might never see each other again. So I did what I thought the moment called for: a chance to say nothing at all, a time to just feel. There was no other choice, in my mind, than to kiss Dr. Uri Nevon.

He held me tightly to his chest as we kissed, a moment that unleashed in me both pent-up longing for Uri and fear of crossing that line.

We stood in the doorway in silence for a moment or two. Finally I sad, "I'm sorry. I shouldn't have done that."

He took my hand. "I'm glad you did. It just...well...it makes things harder."

"Because of Ziva?" I asked. "Because you still love her?" The words had come out more harshly than I'd intended. I sighed and attempted to apologize for my cruelty, but Uri just waved me off. It was he, he had said, that owed me an explanation.

Uri didn't need to clarify anything for me, least of all his feelings for Ziva. I knew he still loved her. And it was really none of my business. But he offered a confession anyway.

He had said that he could deal with the consequences of breaking into the Talpiot tomb again. He could surround himself with rumors about his irresponsible behavior and the disdainful looks of his whispering colleagues. He could even live with the guilt of yet again recruiting Lev to help him break into the tomb because of the boy's willingness to help. But what he couldn't deal with was the heartache of wanting to explore a relationship with me and not being able to.

It was a cruel twist of fate, an irony he grappled with and ultimately was unable to reconcile. He was attracted to an American woman who lived thousands of miles away, but he was still in love with an Israeli woman who had betrayed him and lied to him.

There was no moving on for Uri Nevon. No resolution. No compromise. As long as Ziva walked the earth, there could be no one else.

"Come to America," I'd said impetuously, foolishly, attempting to change his mind. "We'll start a new life together."

"My life, my work, is here," he said. "And your life is in America."

So as we rode west along the highway to Tel Aviv, enroute to the Ben Guiron airport, I couldn't help but reflect on how right he was.

I could be a novelist anywhere in the world, but there was nowhere else I'd rather be than in the City of Brotherly Love. My life was in Philadelphia. My family. My career. My friends. Even Thomas, my dear, sweet ex-husband, was within a half-hour drive. I still loved him, and as long as he walked the earth, I, like Uri, felt there could be no one else.

So entertaining the idea that Uri and I, two people who were in love with other people, could have a life together was frivolous at best. At worst, it would be disastrous. We both knew it, so there was no need to spend any more time discussing it.

We reached the airport and Uri parked the car curbside outside of the departures gate. He retrieved my luggage from the trunk and asked if he could help me carry my bags inside.

I shook my head, seeing no need to make our goodbye last any longer than it had to be. This brief moment would be hard enough. He nodded in agreement.

"I'm very grateful for you, and I care a lot for you," I said. I felt the tears coming, my eyes moistening with emotion, so I quickly added, "And I'm sorry for screwing up your life."

Uri laughed softly and took my hand. "Mara yakiri." *My dear Mara.* "Your apology is unnecessary. I have no regrets."

"Thank you...for everything," I stammered, attempting to quell the sudden hammering of my heart from Uri's touch.

There was a brief pause where neither of us spoke. Uri swayed towards me ever so slightly, a subtle lean of his body as if gauging my receptiveness to a hug or kiss.

A hug would be appropriate, I thought, and far less damaging than a kiss. I gave his neck a tight squeeze and he wrapped his arms around my waist. The embrace was brief; I think we both feared that anything longer might cause us to never want to let go.

I handed the envelope to Uri, the one I had been clutching in my hand since we'd left the hotel.

"Tell him I said goodbye and thank you," I said.

He nodded and took the envelope.

And then I walked away, accepting that some stories aren't meant to be told, some secrets aren't meant to be revealed, and life doesn't always have a happy ending.

EPILOGUE

J *une 2009*
  Dear Lev,
Today is my last day in Jerusalem. My work in your city is complete. I'm going home.

I'm sorry that because of the Sabbath and the early hour that I can't see you one last time and tell you in person how grateful I am for you. You are truly a remarkable young man, and my life has been enriched for knowing you. Had I known about your and Uri's plans to gain access to the tomb, I never would've agreed. I would've walked away. As it is, I feel responsible for putting your life in danger and your future in jeopardy.

Please also accept my deepest gratitude for helping make my story complete. Because of you, I feel that if I wanted to, I could write that best-seller. As it stands now, however, I wouldn't feel right capitalizing on something that you and Uri were primarily responsible for. Everything I accomplished I owe to you. But perhaps one day I'll write the story I wanted to tell.

I wish you the best of luck with your university studies. Stay in school, learn all you can, and I know that you'll find much success in whatever you set your sights on.

Enclosed is ninety shekels. Please mail me another olive wood rosary, the finest one in your store.

● ● ● ●

TODA RABA. THANK YOU very much.
  Lehitra'ot. See you later.
  Shalom,
  Miss Mara

www.ingramcontent.com/pod-product-compliance
Lightning Source LLC
Chambersburg PA
CBHW020639250626
47154CB00008B/2736